Breathless, Marcus pulled his mouth away.

"Well. That's one mystery solved," whispered Tom as he lowered Marcus back to earth, his lips tickling Marcus's ear.

"What do you mean?"

"I wondered if my attraction to you was all in my head" came Tom's husky voice before he thrust his substantial rock-hard groin into Marcus's own arousal. "Apparently not."

WELCOME TO
ⓓREAMSPUN DESIRES

Dear Reader,

Love is the dream. It dazzles us, makes us stronger, and brings us to our knees. Dreamspun Desires tell stories of love featuring your favorite heartwarming heroes, captivating plots, and exotic locations. Stories that make your breath catch and your imagination soar.

In the pages of these wonderful love stories, readers can escape to a world where love conquers all, the tenderness of a first kiss sweeps you away, and your heart pounds at the sight of the one you love.

When you put it all together, you find romance in its truest form.

Love always finds a way.

Elizabeth North

Executive Director
Dreamspinner Press

Brian Lancaster

THE MISSING INGREDIENT

PUBLISHED BY

Published by
DREAMSPINNER PRESS

5032 Capital Circle SW, Suite 2, PMB# 279,
Tallahassee, FL 32305-7886 USA
www.dreamspinnerpress.com

This is a work of fiction. Names, characters, places, and incidents either
are the product of author imagination or are used fictitiously, and any
resemblance to actual persons, living or dead, business establishments,
events, or locales is entirely coincidental.

The Missing Ingredient
© 2018 Brian Lancaster.
Editorial Development by Sue Brown-Moore.

Cover Art
© 2018 Aaron Anderson
aaronbydesign55@gmail.com
Cover content is for illustrative purposes only and any person depicted
on the cover is a model.

Paperback ISBN: 978-1-64108-051-4
Digital ISBN: 978-1-64080-274-2
Library of Congress Control Number: 2017953196
Paperback published August 2018
v. 1.0

Printed in the United States of America
∞
This paper meets the requirements of
ANSI/NISO Z39.48-1992 (Permanence of Paper).

BRIAN LANCASTER is an author of gay romantic fiction in multiple genres, including contemporary, paranormal, fantasy, crime, mystery, and anything else his muse provides. Born in the sleepy South of England, the setting of many of his stories, he moved to Southeast Asia in 1998, where he shares a home with his longtime partner and two of the laziest cats on the planet. Brian Lancaster once believed that writing gay romantic fiction would be easy and cathartic. He also believed in Santa Claus and the Jolly Green Giant. At least he still has fantasies about those two. Born in the rural South of England in a town with its own clock tower and cricket pitch, he moved to Hong Kong in 1998. Life went from calm and curious to fast and furious. On the upside, the people he has since met provide inspiration for a whole new cast of characters in his stories. He also has his long-term, long-suffering partner and two cats to keep him grounded. After winning two short story competitions in 2006 and being published in a compendium, he decided to dive into writing full-length novels. Diving proved to be easy; the challenge has been in treading water and trying to remain afloat. Cynical enough to be classed a curable romantic, he is not seeking an antidote. When not working or writing, he enjoys acting in community theater productions, composing music, hosting pub quizzes, and any socializing that involves Chardonnay. And for the record, he would like to remind all those self-righteous white wine drinkers that White Burgundy, Chablis, and Champagne are still essentially Chardonnays.

Chapter One

FEIGNING sleep, Marcus Vine cracked an eye open when the warm male body next to him rolled away to perch on the side of the bed. Last night's hookup sat there for a moment, his broad back on full display, lowering his head and pushing hands through dark oily locks. An ornately patterned tattoo of curls and thorns and flora decorated well-defined muscles of tanned silken skin. When he stood upright and moved toward the bathroom, his pert muscled backside and thick hairy thighs moved with the easy grace of a feline predator. After hesitating by the bathroom door a moment, he spun around and headed back toward the bed.

The view full frontal now, Marcus ogled the man's sheer physical beauty. Perfect pectorals covered with a dusting of dark moss that trailed down in a line toward the generous cock nestled in a triangular bush of pubic hair. A little too trim actually. Did he manscape down there? And what if he did? Marcus chastised himself. A man should make the most of what he's got. The hunk in question—what was his name again?—plucked his cell phone from the bedside cabinet and scooped up his clothes from the floor before heading back toward the bathroom.

As soon as the door closed, Marcus sat up and checked the time: 8:10. A whole morning before his lunchtime meeting. Part of him wanted to call someone close, a friend back in England to share his exploits with and get a second opinion. But there was no one, not anymore. That used to be the job of Lorraine Bradford—Raine—his best friend since high school. Just thinking about her elicited a pang of sadness. Almost a year to the day, they had lost her in a car accident, and then, at the request of Tom, her widowed husband, he'd agreed to give the family time to heal. Even if he'd never said the words aloud, he'd always believed that he and Raine would be a part of each other's lives into old age.

But that was then, and if working in the restaurant trade had taught him anything, it was the importance of picking yourself up after any setback and moving forward. Nobody else would do it for you.

Perhaps he should make fresh coffee. Then again, maybe the guy would want to escape as soon as he'd finished in the bathroom. Or perhaps his inclination to overuse the word "like" would be just as prevalent in the morning. Why couldn't Marcus meet a normal guy who had beauty, stamina, *and* a modicum of intelligence? Someone like Tom Bradford, who had all of those and more. At least this guy hadn't indicated wanting anything serious. Marcus folded his arms and thought back to the night before.

Hindsight could be a pain in the arse. And not a good one. Alarm bells should have sounded when the conversation on their stroll back to his Manhattan serviced apartment became progressively one-sided. Then again, perhaps bells had already been ringing, but Marcus had been deaf to them, hypnotized by the man's charisma and masculine beauty. Until they had settled back in the apartment, that is, when what's-his-name had continued to bombard him in adolescent enthusiasm with stories about his budding modeling career, his disdain for the amateurism of *America's Next Top Model* and other reality modeling shows, and the various countries he had been to and had yet to visit. At first the excitement had been endearing, almost infectious. And then the man had insisted on talking Marcus through two hundred and twenty-eight professional photographs of himself on his tablet computer. Admittedly some had been stunning, in various costumes, poses, and states of undress, but when he segued into photos of his three pedigree Persian cats, Marcus's ardency had not so much waned as flatlined.

Thursday night drifted into the early hours of Friday morning. And the sex—once they got there— had been at best lackluster. A good word, actually, because the whole encounter lacked any kind of lust. The six-feet-four hunk turned out to be not so much passive as inanimate, rolling over, pushing his face into the pillow, and lying prone. Not once did he respond to kisses on the neck or caresses along the perfect ridge of his back, even to a gentle massage across broad shoulders and down the sides of his torso. Nor did he attempt to reciprocate in any way. So unmoving was he that at one point Marcus wondered if he should check for a pulse. Admittedly, the man—what the hell was his name?—had labeled his sexuality "fluid." Maybe he meant fluid as in a tub of wet cow's liver. Or maybe this was a modern generational thing, some kind of new millennial sacrificial sex. Eventually Marcus had sighed and given up, rolled to the other side of the king-size mattress, and fallen asleep.

But then the hunk had stayed until morning, so what did that mean? Maybe Marcus should turn off the spiteful critic in his head and cut the man—*Freddie*, his name was Freddie—some slack. Having someone that striking by his side couldn't do his budding culinary career any harm. And the fact they were on different continents was absolutely perfect. Skype or phone relationships rocked. And then maybe his friends and workmates would finally get off his case about him being a die-hard one-night-stander. Bite the bullet, he told himself, and ask for Freddie's number as soon as the moment felt right.

When he heard the shower running, he breathed a sigh of relief. Stretching out an arm, he grabbed his mobile phone and thumbed the ringer back on. As he peered at the phone display, he noticed a couple of long-distance missed calls from an unknown number. Ah well, he thought, if it was important they'd phone back.

Half an hour later, togged out in track bottoms and a simple white tee, he heard the bathroom door open.

Olive branch time.

"Coffee?"

"Caffeine's poison. Got guava?"

"Juice?"

"Yeah."

"Sorry, no. There's orange juice in the fridge, I think."

"Fresh squeezed?"

"Probably. Before the manufacturer added sugar and chemicals and shit and poured it into a box."

"No, then. Talk about death by fructose. I'll, like, get something natural on the way to the dance studio. In fact, I should get going."

And suddenly Marcus remembered why they had connected. Not only did the man look after himself physically, but he cared about what went into his body. Yes, maybe this was somebody he could have around— albeit at a distance.

"So before you go, Freddie, I wondered if I could get—"

"What did you just call me?"

"Freddie," said Marcus, faltering. "Isn't that your name?"

"*Oh*. Em. *Gee*. That is *so* not my name."

"I'm sorry. It was loud in the club last night. I must have misheard."

"Repeat after me. Fair."

"Sorry?"

"Fair!"

"Oh. Fair."

"Red."

"Red."

"Deek."

"Uh, deek."

"Fer-ed-dique."

"Fereddique."

Are you fucking kidding me?

"Three syllables, not two. Emphasis on the second. Was going to run with *Red*, but that's, like, too tacky and common. Now whenever you read the name on a billboard, you'll know it's me. So what were you about to offer? You, like, asked if you could get me something."

Marcus stared at his phone display, praying for divine intervention. "Can I get you a cab?"

"Heck no," said Fereddique, effortlessly pulling on a chestnut corduroy jacket and flipping his ebony curls back from the collar. "I'll walk. Studio's, like, only ten blocks from here. That's why I stayed over."

Aaaaand the cruelest cut of all. Oblivious to the coup de grace, Fereddique appeared completely at ease, finishing off the ensemble by deftly tying an eggplant wool scarf around his throat, doubtless to ward off the chill February air.

As soon as he'd finished, he paused to scrutinize Marcus before coming over and pulling him into the briefest of hugs, the kind of antiseptic endearment Marcus's pious aunt favored. With a step back, Fereddique left his hands on Marcus's forearms.

"I'll see myself out," he said, smiling at Marcus before letting him go and heading for the door. About to depart, he poked his head back into the apartment and said, "And good luck with your cooking thing, Magnus."

Marcus accompanied the closing of the door with an indignant huff. Not that he minded the faux pas with his name—he'd made the same mistake—but *cooking thing*? Back in London he had made a name for himself as a rising culinary virtuoso. Okay, so nowhere near the same league as Anthony Bourdain or Gordon Ramsay—neither did he want to be—but Marcus had resurrected traditional British recipes using organic, untreated, and fresh local ingredients. His grandparents—Gaelic and Celtic on his father's side and Anglo-Saxon on his mother's—had trained him to whip up a range of almost forgotten dishes. During college and beyond, Marcus had spent weekends scouring bookstores and markets for old recipe books, and worked hard to bring them up-to-date and, moreover, make them healthy. Now both of his London-based Old Country restaurants had achieved hard-won critical acclaim in the eyes of the capital's fine diners and the ever-judgmental media.

Not bad for a thirty-year-old. And if his manager, Tina, ever got her way, he would be strutting his stuff on a cable network television cooking channel. So far, however, that was one battle she had not won and, if he had his way, never would. Marcus enjoyed his anonymity, having his minor celebrity status confined to the restaurant or an occasional newspaper article in one of the national dailies.

"Breathe and let it go, Vine," he told himself aloud. As usual, he had a split second of disappointment that came and went like a lick of sherbet, before comforting thoughts settled in. Apart from being moderately successful, he still had everything to live for, nothing and no one tying him down. Not anymore. Maybe the solution was to stop paying attention to his friends and colleagues, most of whom translated their shackled lives of debt, petty arguments, sleepless nights, and nappies into the more acceptable term of wedded bliss. Maybe he should get a dog or a cat? But then apartment living would not be fair to them, especially with the hours that Marcus worked. A goldfish, then? Self-sufficient, no poop to scoop, no yapping or meowing, and something his neighbor Ruth might be happy to feed while he spent time away. A goldfish for companionship. One-night stands for sex. Done deal.

Thirty minutes later, after he'd washed and dressed, his telephone rang. Tina's name and face popped up on the display. Not a good photo with her scowling at the camera—she had been with him the day he bought the device; hers had been the first photo he'd taken—but it

tended to make him smile before he answered. Ignoring
the trill, Marcus took his coffee and strolled over to the
floor-to-ceiling window, where he perched on the arm
of the sofa before taking the call.

"Mrs. Adebayo-Cruickshank," he said, and then
took a sip of the coffee, nodding his approval to the
Manhattan skyline. "How are you this morning?"

Tina Adebayo had been his business partner for
the best part of the past five years. Second-generation
Nigerian, she stood at an intimidating six-two. In
meetings, she mesmerized. A razor-sharp mind together
with her deep, rich voice never failed to widen the eyes
of any opponent. Always on the same side of the table
as her—thank heavens—Marcus had come to enjoy
watching the blanching of faces opposite him.

"Oh my God," she groaned. "I still can't get used
to hearing that name. Doesn't sound right, does it?"

Tina and her longtime boyfriend, Mel, had finally
taken the plunge last year. Marcus had catered the small
wedding reception, not something he would normally
offer, but for Tina he had happily made an exception.

"I don't know. I quite like it, actually. Has a nice
ring to it."

"Anyway, don't get me sidetracked," she interrupted.
"What time did you leave the club last night?"

"Not long after you, around ten thirty."

"Uh-huh. And did you get a good workout with
poster boy?"

"Who? Oh, don't even," he sighed, and rolled his
eyes for effect even though she couldn't see him.

"But that chunk-of-hunk was so—Oh. Em. Gee!"

"Fereddique. His name is Fereddique. And please
don't ever use that acronym again in conversation
with me."

"Really? But he was built like an Aberdeen Angus rib eye steak."

"Tina, if I had to compare last night's liaison to a particular food, it would not be beef. I would pick uncooked, unseasoned, flavorless tofu. Sat unmoving on a plate like cold blancmange. Packing lube and condoms turned out to be completely unnecessary. If only I weren't so shallow when it came to my type."

"Finally."

"What does that mean?"

"I can't remember the quote exactly, but it goes along the lines that having both happiness and beauty would simply be too good to be true."

While Marcus mulled the words over, Tina clarified. "Walter Benjamin, I think. German poet and critic. Anyway, down to business."

"No, hang on a moment. You can't just throw out bumper sticker philosophy like that and expect me to be quiet. What do you mean?"

"I mean you go for a certain… type. And from what I can tell, they're rarely keepers."

Oh Lord, thought Marcus. Here we go again. First lecture of the day. "So what are you telling me? Tall, dark, good-looking, and fit are bad things now?"

"Of course not. But you could try for something a little less…."

"Less what?"

"Less—shallow."

"You think he was shallow?"

"As a mouse's grave. Unless you're going to tell me otherwise."

The snuffled chuckle down the phone at his hesitation sent a trickle of annoyance through him. Why did everybody find him so transparent?

"So what's on the agenda today?" he said irritably. "Let me guess. More endless meetings and bear-in-a-cage appearances."

"Four small meetings left for early next week, with the big one on Wednesday. And yes, still awaiting confirmation, but you possibly have a cooking demo Monday morning on a local cable network channel, where you will unashamedly plug your soon-to-be-released cookbook, your London success story, and mention the likelihood of opening a restaurant here in the nation's darling. And tomorrow evening we have dinner with the main investment candidates. You won't be expected to rustle anything up at that one, but I do need you to bring your best game—"

"Strip poker?"

"And try to appear charming, sociable, and above all marketable."

"Can't I just cook?"

"That could be arranged. But I should let you know that Kurt Bruckmeyer has specifically asked to be seated next to you."

"Has he now?"

Kurt Bruckmeyer was the twenty-seven-year-old son of Arnold Bruckmeyer, New York socialite and billionaire. He had caught Kurt checking him out a couple of times across the boardroom table. Not that Kurt was his type—too waspish and formal, too thin and groomed, the kind of man who looked completely at home in a tightly buttoned-up designer suit but awkward in anything even vaguely casual. Who ironed pleats into their jeans these days, for goodness' sake? Still, if push came to shove and it helped his budding career, he could take one for the team.

"Wednesday's meeting is the biggie. We'll know by the end of that one if we have the big green apple light. And then we'll catch the first flight home Thursday morning."

"Thank the heavens."

"I wouldn't count your blessings just yet. You've got an interview with lifestyle journo Donald Kitter from the *Observer*, and the agents have come up with half-a-dozen potentials for your UK Birmingham site. We'll need to arrange a trip soon. So make the most of your downtime in America's very own Elysium."

America's Elysium. New York. Still with the phone stuck to his ear, he scanned the room. His investors had spared no expense in romancing him, giving him the star treatment. And of course he was flattered—who wouldn't be? The beige, gray, and gleaming chrome two-bedroom apartment in the East Village—stylish, spacious, and tastefully furnished—must have been showcased in a real estate magazine or six. On two floor-to-ceiling windowed sides of the main room, the city views alone, both day and night, were nothing short of stunning. Framed in the narrower window, beyond old and new buildings he couldn't name, flowed the East River, and through the main window that faced north, the instantly recognizable Empire State Building. Sometimes he wished he had someone to share it all with—but then again, maybe not. Eight days away from home and more to come, he ached to be back to the routine of the kitchen. Both sous-chefs—handpicked by Marcus—were perfectly capable of managing on their own, but punters who had waited months for a booking often wanted a glimpse of the man himself. And if Marcus was going to be completely candid, he loved the attention. On his own terms, on his own turf, in his own world. Absently, he took another sip of his coffee.

"What are you drinking?"

"Coffee."

Down the phone came a sharp intake of breath.

"Not that wonderful spicy Kenyan concoction?"

"What else?"

"Bugger. Wish I was there now."

"Come up, then. You're only a floor down."

"In a one-bedroom shoe cupboard."

"Stop complaining. You could have stayed here. There are two bedrooms. What do I need with two bedrooms?"

"You're the talent, sweetie. Not me. And anyway, you'd only end up moaning about my constant stream of telephone calls," she said as she grunted, clearly taking some effort to do something at her end. "Americans like to impress their stars, not the help. Hence the palatial suite. We ought to market that coffee mix, you know? And I just love the way you go about preparing everything. So effortless. Would look great on—"

"Television. Honestly, Tina, you're as see-through as shrink-wrap."

"Only looking out for you. You're thirty. Ramsay wasn't that much older when he opened his own restaurant and stepped in front of the cameras. At a time when the viewing public were hungry to see how professionals worked in the kitchen. Nowadays those types of cooking shows are ten a penny no matter where you are in the world."

"And your point is?"

"The public wants newcomers who have something fresh and original to dazzle them with, people who go one step further. Like Heston Blumenthal. And if you don't crank up your career now, you might miss the boat."

"Why do you think I'm in New York?"

"You'll still be in the kitchen."

"I'm a chef. That's where I'm meant to be."

"Darling. With your good looks and charm, you need to be in front of the camera."

Oh heavens, thought Marcus, here we go again. "My good looks and charm couldn't even get me laid last night. Move it along, Tina."

Right then his phone buzzed with another number.

"What's that noise?"

"Another call coming through."

"I'll let you go, then. Be ready at ten thirty."

Before Marcus had a chance to pick up the call—once again the display only provided the single word "unknown"—the caller rang off. He issued a deep irritated breath, which froze and turned to wonderment while he stared out the window at the mix of iconic new architecture and historical buildings. All too often his English associates had smiled politely at their American colleagues, who crowed on about their pint-size heritage and culture, but just standing there looking at the nouveau classic New York skyline took Marcus's breath away. No question about it, his life was charmed. Even if he did bemoan being away from home, working extraordinarily long hours, and feeling a very occasional pang about not having someone to share his life with, everything he touched businesswise seemed to turn to gold.

Maybe he would have liked to have his family more present in his life, to share his successes with. But Colin and Debs—they had given him strict instructions as soon as he was old enough never to use "Mum and Dad" labels—were nothing short of an inspiration. Both in their fifties, they still had their careers in the theater that kept them busy, still loved each other like nobody else he knew. Fuck, their love for each other could inspire a best-selling self-help book. Not that they didn't love him to bits too, but their passion for each other transcended everything and continued on after their sole offspring had left the nest. And if he ever needed them, he knew unshakably that they would be there for him.

And that was just how he wanted things, wasn't it?

Before Raine passed, he had wanted more, would have seriously considered a family of his own, with the man of his dreams by his side. Not impossible, because Raine's family had been the perfect model, a little piece of heaven, a sanctuary in an unpredictable world. And ironically, the only man who had ever come anywhere close to his ideal had been Tom Bradford, Raine's husband and father to their two daughters.

Just then the phone rang again and Marcus quickly tapped his thumb on the screen. If this was somebody trying to sell him anything, he would give them a piece of his mind.

"May I speak to Marcus Vine?" came the professional voice of an older woman, a voice that sounded vaguely accented, French perhaps.

"Speaking."

"Marcus, this is Cherry Labouche from *Paris Match*. Were you aware that this year's *Michelin Guide* is being published today?"

"I was aware it was this month. But I thought it wasn't until next week."

When the possible implications behind the call finally hit him, he took a deep breath and held on tight.

"Yes, well, our publication is able to call in a few favors where publishers are concerned. So I am sure you will be extremely pleased to hear that your Edgware Road Old Country restaurant has been nominated for a Michelin

Rising Star Award, which means that you may very well qualify for one star in the near future. I wondered if you would be interested in providing an exclusive interview for our magazine? With photographs, of course, and the article to be published next month?"

Michelin star? After Marcus had pulled himself together, he accepted—of course—on the proviso that Cherry talk to his manager to arrange details, even though the next person he picked the phone up to call would be that very one.

Yes, he thought, so life had thrown him a couple of curveballs over the past year. But then someone up there clearly wanted him to be successful. So what if he didn't have all the other trappings life gave others?

Marcus Vine was going places.

Everything else could wait.

Chapter Two

EVEN from a distance, Marcus could tell Tina had a hangover. Few women he knew lurched. All in black with a scarlet-tinted fringe of wild black hair poking out from beneath a charcoal woolen hat, she resembled a pallbearer rather than a business partner. Three weeks before, on their flight back from JFK, for this trip they had arranged for him to park the car at her apartment block before walking the short distance to the mainline station. He'd have been happy to drive, but Tina was not a good passenger and regularly suffered from travel sickness. On top of that, she had cautioned him about Sunday, about her birthday and her hunch that Mel had planned something special—which would entail copious amounts of alcohol. Marcus smiled. On the positive side, Tina plus hangover equaled no-nonsense negotiations. Straight to the point. No conjecture, no pleasantries or procrastination—no bullshit. Plenty of coffee and aspirin. And the asshole landlord in Birmingham whose property they were in negotiations to rent, to open the first of his restaurants in the Midlands, needed some tough talk. Prime location aside, they would need to spend at least another hundred and fifty thousand to bring the place up to code.

"Before you even think about lecturing me, I need fast-food ballast," she croaked in confirmation, not even slowing as she caught up with him. "The stodgier and greasier, the better. And lots of it. And nuclear-strength coffee. Triple shot espresso bare-bones minimum."

"Do we have time?" he asked.

"There's a 9:20 fast train to Victoria. Delays aside, we'll be in Birmingham before midday. Plenty of time."

"All for a one-hour meeting. We should have done this by video con."

"You know that's not an option. I need to see the whites of this dickhead's eyes before I nail the bastard to the table. But I need bulk and a train nap before I do battle."

Marcus chuckled. "Then lead the way."

Since Raine's death, Tina had, by default, become his go-to female friend for matters of the heart. Marcus had grown up with Raine, and her guidance had been gentle, measured, and above all, feminine. Tina's business advice was usually brutally sound, and using the same approach for emotional counsel, especially with her short-fuse patience, rarely left him entirely satisfied.

So rather than engage Tina in any meaningful conversation, Marcus strode alongside in respectful silence. When they reached the garishly decorated fast-food outlet and Marcus pushed the door inward, he was met with a wall of noise. "What the hell…?"

"Oh shit, yes," said Tina, next to him. "Local teachers in the borough are on strike over school funding, something organized by the teacher's union. A couple of schools have had to close their doors for the day. Poor parents have to keep their little cherubs occupied somehow. So what else are you going to do with them? Don't worry, I'll get takeout. You wait here."

As he stood there amid the squealing, swirling cattle roundup of youngsters, one of them broke from the pack and collided with his leg. When he peered down, a powder-pink-tutu-clad girl with familiar wild brown hair stared up at him, full of a wide-eyed innocence that only kids could pull off. As he hiked in a breath, a pang of sadness crept over him, and he realized how much she resembled her late mother: the cuteness when she leaned her head to one side to produce a smile that could stop traffic, the absent way she placed a tiny finger across her lips. It dawned on him how much he missed his goddaughters.

"Uncle Marc, Uncle Marc," called Charlotte, holding her hands up to him as though she had fully expected him to be there. "Look at me. I'm a princess today."

"Hello, Charlie," said Marcus, putting his case on the floor and lifting Charlotte into the crest of his right arm. She had grown a little in the intervening months but was still manageable. "To me you're a princess every day."

"Not yesterday. Yesterday I was girl pirate. Because it was Ranjit's birthday party and he got to choose. I had a big brown hat with three corners," she said, pointing to her head. "And a white feather. But we had to lose and get taken prisoner because Ranjit said pirates always lose and get taken prisoner. They wanted to tie us up together round the tree in Ranjit's garden, but his mummy said it was too cold, and they didn't have any rope anyway. Stupid soldiers."

"If I'd been there, nobody would have tried to tie my little princess up."

"Where *have* you been, Uncle Marc?"

Out of the mouths of babes. Trust the little one to make him feel instantly guilty. Marcus scanned the restaurant to find who had brought his goddaughter with them.

"Uncle Marc has been really busy, princess. Who are you here with? Grandma?"

"No. Daddy and Katie," she said, wriggling out of his grasp and, once back on the ground, grabbing his hand. "Come say hello."

Marcus felt the ice-cold sting of angst in his stomach. At the funeral, Tom had asked for a time-out, time to be left alone to get the family back on their feet. And Marcus had agreed—what else could he do?—and had waited for a call from Tom to say that things had settled. A call that never came. Marcus interpreted the silence to mean they didn't need him.

Then again, seeing Charlotte had lifted his spirits. And realistically, the funeral had been just over a year ago. Absently, he wondered how they'd all coped over Christmas, the first without Raine. He'd sent presents but had heard nothing in return. Maybe Tom would be more at peace this time. At least they were in a public place and he had Tina in his corner. What harm could it do to pop over and say hello? Before he knew what was happening, Charlie had dragged him to a small booth at the corner of the restaurant.

Katie looked well enough except for her outfit: a mini jean jacket over a red frilly top with the seams on the outside—put on back to front—and bright green leggings. Raine would have been horrified, but apparently Tom let the girls wear whatever they wanted. Ketchup blotches on her hand, she had been in the process of eating a french fry when she looked up and caught sight of Marcus. Another thing Raine had forbidden: fast food. Even though he could not make out the flyby of emotions that crossed seven-year-old Katie's face, somewhere in there was relief. And then, when her gaze flicked to the man on her left, he saw why.

Tom sat at the table, hunched forward. Had they been on the street, Marcus might well have walked past without recognizing him. Unshaven and a little rumpled were minor things. The gauntness of his usually strong features spoke of undernourishment, and his fixed gaze focused somewhere outside the front window, somewhere beyond the horizon.

Eight years ago Marcus had been introduced to Tom Bradford, right wing for a Sunday soccer team. At the game's end, handsome Tom had moved toward them like a weary warrior leaving the battlefield. Signs of the hard-fought encounter had clung to him, slick mud glistening down one side of his body from where he had made a sliding tackle, the muddied sock of one hairy leg rolled down to the ankle, dark hair damp with rain and sweat plastered to his forehead and cheeks. Fists bunched at his hips, his heavy breaths producing steamy plumes, his large chest rising and falling…. Marcus had been instantly smitten.

Sitting hunched there today, Tom Bradford bore little resemblance to the Tom Bradford of yesteryear.

"Tom?"

Hypnotized by whatever had caught his attention out beyond the window, the man continued staring into the distance.

"Daddy," chastised Charlotte, squeezing in next to her father. "Uncle Marcus is here."

Somehow the voice of his youngest daughter pulled his attention away, and he turned to peer down at her, puzzled, until her words sank in and he raised his eyes to Marcus. The tiredness in that first glassy stare broke Marcus's heart. But like his older daughter, Tom recovered quickly and looked genuinely happy.

"Marcus," he said, sitting up in his seat. "Nice to see you. How are things?"

"I'm—I'm well. How are you?"

Tom grinned brightly then, and the old attraction that Marcus had harbored throughout the years resurfaced. "We're fine. Well, work is pretty full-on. But we're doing fine, aren't we, girls? Coping, you know? Grab a seat."

When Tom indicated the bench seat opposite, Marcus thought he noticed his hand shaking slightly. "Tom, I'd love to, but I'm about to catch the train to Birmingham. My colleague is just getting her breakfast fix."

Tom's stoic grin and nod of resignation cut Marcus to the bone. After a quick glance over his shoulder to see if Tina loomed nearby and catching sight of her hat in a long queue two from the front, he sat down.

"What the hell," said Marcus. "Five minutes can't hurt."

The problem was that after twelve months, apart from the usual pleasantries, Marcus had no idea what to say or ask. Fortunately Charlotte provided a commentary.

"Uncle Marcus has been very busy, Daddy. He's been in the newspaper and all. Grandma showed us."

Marcus chuckled. So he hadn't been completely written off by the remaining Bradford clan. Without thinking, he picked up a clean paper napkin and offered it to Katie, pointing out the spill on the back of her hand. "That's right, Charlie. We're looking to open a restaurant in New York City. Do you know where that is, Katie?"

"Duh," she replied, swiping at the stains before giving him the world-weary look so reminiscent of her late mother. "Everybody knows where New York City is. Even Charlie."

"America."

"Ah, but on which coast of America?"

Katie narrowed her eyes at him then, remembering an old game they used to play, when he helped her to revise for one or another of her school tests.

"I'll give you a clue. Strictly speaking, America doesn't have a north or south coast."

"South coast," shouted Charlie.

"No, Charlie," said Katie, grimacing at her sister. "It's either east or west."

"West," guessed Charlie.

"East Coast," said Katie, and then to show she hadn't just guessed, added, "same as Washington and Boston."

"Well done, Katie," said Marcus, nodding and smiling. "Maybe one day in the future Uncle Marcus can—"

He stopped short then when a sudden wave of sad realization overcame him. Tom had made things clear between them. There would be no more direct contact with either Tom or his goddaughters. His smile slipped and instead he peered down at his hands.

"The girls miss you, Marcus," said Tom, as though reading his thoughts.

"I miss you all too. But I wasn't sure if you were ready…."

He didn't know how to finish the sentence, and Tom gave no sign that he understood what he was trying to say.

"I wasn't sure I was welcome yet."

But Tom didn't hear, his attention drawn from the table to take in someone hovering over them all. When Marcus turned, Tina stood there, as daunting as ever, curiously studying the group. Marcus stood and quickly introduced her. After an all too hasty farewell to Tom and the girls, they left.

All the way to the station, the guilty feeling inside him grew. He had a duty, he reminded himself, as godfather to Raine's children. Both she and Tom had persuaded him to take on the role, even though he had balked at the idea when first suggested. And one thing Marcus Vine never did was shy from duty. Nobody in this world was perfect—he had his fair share of faults, but turning from duty was not one of them. By the time he reached the station, he knew exactly what to do.

"Would you mind going and getting the tickets?" he asked Tina, who had managed to finish both coffee and breakfast burger on the walk to the station. "I really need to make a call."

Tucked away in the entrance doorway, away from the sound of traffic and other distractions, Marcus pulled out his mobile phone. After all this time, he still had all their telephone numbers. He found the one he wanted and dialed.

"Hello. Is that Moira Bradford?"

"Speaking." The voice sounded polite but strained, as though she expected the caller to launch into a sales spiel.

"This is Marcus. Marcus Vine."

"Oh. Marcus. Hello. Nice to hear from you. I— what can I help you with?"

"It's more the other way around, actually. I bumped into Tom and the girls in Toasties on the high street. Having breakfast."

Marcus paused to let the words sink in.

"Oh" came the monosyllabic reply, all Moira could apparently muster.

"Moira, is everything okay? Only Tom looked—" said Marcus, faltering because he didn't know how to diplomatically voice what he needed to say. Eventually he breathed a deep sigh and said what he thought. "He looked pretty bloody dreadful, to be brutally honest."

"Oh heavens, Marcus" came the defeated voice down the phone, so unlike the strong and opinionated character who Marcus had come to know and, more often than not, dislike. "I'm doing everything I can, honestly I am. But between John and Tom, there aren't enough hours in the day to—but Tom's just about managing to hold everything together."

"Moira, do you think it would be okay if I pop round and see him tonight? I want to offer my help in whatever way I can."

Marcus wasn't exactly sure of the barely audible sound that came down the phone. It sounded like a relieved sob.

"I think that would be a lovely gesture. I know things were said at the funeral. Tom doesn't handle stress well. And I know that doesn't excuse him. But since then I'm convinced he regrets what he asked for, even if he's too proud to admit it. And even more than that, he hates himself for losing your friendship."

"It's okay, Moira. I think I understand. And I'm as much to blame. I should have been more thick-skinned, should have got back in touch. As godfather to the girls, I have a duty to them. And so far I've been missing in their lives. If anyone's been reprehensible, it's me."

"Do you want me to take the girls tonight? So that the two of you can speak privately?"

"No," said Marcus. "I'm going to be in Birmingham today. By the time I get to the house, I'm sure the girls will be getting ready for bed. And I want them to see me too, to understand that their Uncle Marc hasn't deserted them. But I'll call you when I'm there so that we tally schedules, if that's okay?"

"Of course. You've no idea how relieved that makes me feel. More than anything, my son needs a friend right now, Marcus."

Chapter Three

THAT evening, Marcus managed to mask his dismay when the door opened to the Bradford family's modest two-bedroom terraced house. Engaged on his mobile phone, Tom was wearing the same jeans and rumpled rugby shirt, and had probably neither been to the office nor showered. And once again, his face had that exhausted expression, a general tired confusion, so out of character for this usually in-control man. On the bright side, Moira must have called him, because he appeared really pleased, if a little distracted, to see Marcus standing on the doorstep.

"I come bearing gifts," said Marcus, holding up a shopping bag.

On arriving back from an extremely frustrating and fruitless meeting, he had purchased fresh pasta and other natural ingredients from the organic supermarket next to the station before picking his car up and driving straight to Tom's. If he could do nothing else for his inherited family, he could at least cook them a decent, healthy meal.

Tom mumbled something inaudible to the caller before opening the door wide. Marcus had never really warmed to their modern new-build house, but Tom had bought the place with cash when they first married, fully intending to upscale to one more substantial as soon as children came along. Then economic times plummeted and Tom's construction business suffered along with the rest of those in the country, making competition tough and profit margins thin. Despite mild protests from Raine, offers of handouts from his parents had been humored but emphatically rejected. Tom Bradford made his own way in this world, thank you very much. Although he had continued to squirrel money away for the future, they'd never quite had enough or found the time to upgrade.

Marcus stepped across the threshold and tripped over a plastic toy pony discarded on the hallway carpet. When the door closed behind him, odors of sugary cereals and stale food instantly assaulted Marcus's sense of smell. By the front door, Katie's Disney backpack sat discarded on the floor next to an untidy pile of school coats, which had once hung in their regular place on the coatrack. Toys strewn along the floor of the hallway and living room looked as though they had been there for days, maybe weeks. Raine had always been house-proud, even with two hyperactive kids to clear up after.

Marcus lowered his shopping bag onto the countertop of the open kitchen. Signs of the girls' tea—an empty can of spaghetti hoops and a half loaf of sliced bread—sat next to the toaster. Unwashed dishes and pans overflowed from the sink onto the work surface. Even the kitchen floor was mottled with crumbs and splashes of food. Marcus had to stop his natural, professional inclination to roll up his sleeves and tackle the mess. Instead he moved to the middle of the living area and waited for Tom to speak.

"Sorry," said Tom, a pained expression squeezing his features as he followed Marcus's gaze. "I'll get around to that later. The girls were exhausted. They've been at home all day running amok. I've already put them to bed."

"You have?" said Marcus, unable to mask his disappointment. He could always converse better with Tom when either Raine or the girls were around. But tonight was important, and he needed to get his act together, to keep his focus. "No problem. Better probably. Means we can chat without being disturbed."

"Come sit down," said Tom, moving quickly to the main couch and tossing several toys onto the floor to make space for Marcus. "Can I get you something?"

"Not yet. Let's have a chat first."

Tom nodded and seated himself across from Marcus. Rather than covering pleasantries again, Marcus dived into the conversation.

"How are you balancing work with caring for the girls?"

Although fleeting, the pain crossing Tom's face was clear. "It's been tough. I won't lie. I've missed a lot of work and Pete, my partner, has been a star taking up the slack. But he can't keep doing that forever, and moreover we need more business coming through the door. Otherwise we're all out of a job. That's my specialty. Going out, meeting clients, and getting the work in."

"Who's helping you? With the girls?"

"Mum, mainly."

"Anyone else?"

"Our neighbor, Olive, takes them in sometimes after school if I'm running late. And the mother of one of Katie's friends, Mrs. Kelley. They've both been great," said Tom, looking levelly at Marcus. "I'm doing all I can, I really am, Marcus. But…." Tom faltered, so unlike him.

"But?"

"Oh God, I haven't even told Mum." He stood abruptly and went to the small dining table, where, from a pile of papers, he pulled out a brown envelope. When Marcus spotted the Social Services name across the envelope, an involuntary icy shiver ran through him. In silence, he read the carefully worded yet coldly official language about having received a claim indicating that the children might be in danger of neglect and advising him of a visit from a local social worker the following Wednesday.

"I can't lose them too, Marcus."

While still reading, Marcus had been unprepared for the sudden eruption of emotions that ripped from inside, part anger at the faceless and nameless threat and part rage at himself for having deserted Tom and the girls when they needed him most. Without thinking, he shot up from the sofa and spat at the letter.

"Over my dead body. Over my *fucking* dead body are they taking the girls into care. You're a good father, Tom. Anybody can see that. Who the fuck do they think they are? And what kind of an arsehole would have reported—"

But as quickly as the emotional tsunami rushed in, as he peered down at Tom, his common sense kicked in. He stopped, sat back down, and took a few steadying breaths before continuing calmly but assertively. Many times in his restaurant kitchen, this tactic in times of crisis had borne dividends.

"Tom, this is not going to happen. I promise you, okay? But we need to stay positive and, more importantly, get organized. This is all fixable. Where's Raine's scheduling board? It used to be on the fridge."

One of Lorraine's qualities—and she had many—had been her ability to meticulously organize the lives of the people around her. Nothing ever slipped through the net. For the girls, she had used a simple magnetized whiteboard with a crisscross of lines to organize their time; after-school activities; anything they needed to bring to class; weekend parties; and more importantly, which of the adults would be responsible for what. Without ever telling her, Marcus had been so impressed with the way Raine had oiled the wheels of her family's lives that he had adopted the same method to organize a staff rota in each of his restaurants.

Tom returned with the board—still covered with Lorraine's colorful handwriting—a handful of pens, and a damp cloth. Marcus understood without asking. How could Tom bear to stare at his late wife's handwriting on full display every day? Of course he had hidden the board away. Just how much had this poor man suffered alone trying to put on a front of normalcy for his girls?

"Can you get Moira on the phone, on speaker preferably? Let's work out the girls' schedule together."

Moira answered after one ring. Marcus half suspected she had been waiting for the call. With Marcus's schedule allowing him to be available early in the week, they managed to get the next four weeks plugged in. Between Tom and Moira, they detailed all of the girls' after-school activities and special events onto the board. One thing Raine had never done, but something Marcus insisted upon, was writing emergency contact numbers for each of them, including the neighbor, Olive, and Mrs. Kelley. Once it was completed and back in pride of place, Marcus took a photo of the board on his smartphone.

After wishing Moira good night, Marcus turned his attention to Tom. His features had visibly relaxed.

"Okay, mate," said Marcus. "Now you need to do *me* a favor."

"What's that?"

"Go have a shower and a shave. You look like the walking dead. And while you're gone, I'm going to cook up some food."

"I'm not hungry."

"Who said it was for you?"

Tom snorted and shook his head but headed toward the stairs. Before he hit the first step, though, he turned back to Marcus. "Don't touch the dishes. I'll sort the kitchen out when I come down."

"Go and shower," ordered Marcus.

Like a sprinter anticipating the starting gun, Marcus waited for the bathroom door to close, his signal to rush to clean up. Cleanliness and cooking went hand in hand, and he would not even open his shopping bag until the dishes were done and the kitchen surfaces were spotless. First off, though, he set about finding the girls' toy box and clearing all the toys away. Afterward, he got out the carpet sweeper to get rid of the worst of the dirt on the carpet—he wouldn't vacuum while the girls slept. Finally, once he heard the shower going, he cleaned the kitchen floor before setting out a pan of boiling water for the pasta and cooked the sauce, cleaning everything as he went. On many occasions he had offered to cook for the family, so he knew his way around their kitchen like an old hand.

By the time Tom trod gently onto the bottom stair, Marcus had two plates of carbonara, slices of garlic bread, two small bowls of garden salad with a simple lemon, balsamic, and garlic dressing, and two bottles of chilled beer sitting on the dining table. In between cooking, he had also made simple but healthy pack lunches for the girls and Tom, and left them in the fridge. Clean-shaven and in a simple combination of fresh tee and baggy sweatpants, Tom looked incredible, a lot more like the man Marcus had admired all those years ago. When Tom spoke, he had to rip his gaze away.

"Marcus," he said, stopping and looking first around the room and then at the table. "I told you I—"

"I cook. You eat. Now shut up and sit down with me. If you can't eat the food, then just drink the beer."

For someone who claimed not to be hungry, Tom polished off everything on his plate with enthusiasm. By ten o'clock they leaned back together on the sofa, watching the rerun of a soccer game. Man United versus Liverpool. Neutral territory. Tom even chipped in when Marcus provided a commentary about a certain player's performance. Somewhere not too far below the surface, the real Tom was still there.

When Raine had been alive, she and Tom had come to an agreement that when there was a football match on the television, she could go out for drinks with her girlfriends. Marcus, classed as one of the girls, had been included in the invite but had always been conflicted because he also wanted to know how the game was going. On one occasion, when Marcus's team had been playing, and without any prompting from Marcus, Tom had sent him text messages providing updates on the score. This had been a small gesture but one that had always stuck in Marcus's mind.

During the commercials, Marcus sat back into the sofa and went over what they'd agreed, partly to remind himself but also because doing so systematically appeared to relax Tom. A second beer and Tom was almost back to his old self. Only as the game ended did Marcus dare to touch on a topic he had been avoiding all evening.

"Tom. At the funeral—"

"Christ, Marcus. I'm sorry. I should have called you before now, believe me—"

"But do you really believe that Raine was seeing someone?"

"No," said Tom. Marcus regretted having brought the topic up then, but after Tom scrubbed his face with his hands a few times, he carried on. "I honestly didn't know what to believe. At the time, the police wouldn't tell me anything. Just the name of the other person who died in the car along with her."

"Damian Stone."

"You remembered?"

"Not something I could easily forget. I've been racking my brains to think if she'd ever mentioned him before. But the truth is she hadn't. Ask any of my staff—I have a bloody good head for the names."

"Turns out they did yoga together. Lesson was even up on her board still, morning session. And now that I think about it, she used to laugh about some bloke called Stoner—remember thinking what an odd nickname that was."

"Stoner? The other passenger was Stoner?"

Even Marcus had heard Raine laugh about a guy called Stoner, who cracked jokes and made inappropriate noises during sometimes overserious yoga sessions.

"So they were on the way to yoga when it happened? I thought you said something about the accident happening on the M25."

"Yes, the accident happened afterwards."

"So where were they heading?"

"No idea. They'd been talking about joining a different outfit. They both found their existing one a bit stuck-up. Maybe they were headed there. But to be honest, Marcus, it doesn't matter now anyway. Nothing's going to bring her back."

"If you say so," said Marcus, a trace of doubt in his voice.

"What are you doing here, Uncle Marc?" came a young voice from the stairs. Katie stood there in her SpongeBob SquarePants pajamas, bleary-eyed, her auburn hair sticking up in all the wrong places.

"Go back to bed, princess. Me and Uncle Marcus are having a grown-up conversation."

"What are you doing with Mummy's Play Planner?" she asked, folding her arms adorably.

"Her what, Katie?" asked Marcus.

"It's what Raine used to call the organizer," said Tom. "Uncle Marc and I have been planning out the next few weeks' activities. Figuring out who will pick you girls up and drop you off. So that you can still attend all your activities."

"Is Uncle Marcus going to be coming to see us more often now?"

Although he remained silent then, Marcus could sense Tom turn his way. The words, the pledge, needed to come from him.

"Yes, Katie," said Marcus, noticing a very faint wheeze from the little girl. "I'm going to be here lots, as long as you, Charlotte, and Daddy want me here. Did you need your inhaler? I think I saw it on the table."

She smiled then and plodded into the living room.

"How's the maths coming along?" he asked, which got him a roll of the eyes reminiscent of her late mother.

"Numbers. And I hate numbers. They don't seem to make sense."

"Well, then," said Marcus, "mission number one. We're just going to have to make them make sense to you, aren't we?"

"If you say so," she said, going over and getting the small blue L-shaped inhaler. She turned and smiled at him then, but it didn't quite reach her eyes, telling him that he wasn't forgiven yet. "Charlotte will be happy to see you, to get things back to normal."

Well, not normal, perhaps, thought Marcus, but maybe a new kind of normal.

After Katie had taken herself back upstairs, Marcus and Tom washed the dishes together in companionable silence before Marcus made his excuse to leave. Tom walked Marcus to the front door and they stood together unspeaking for a moment. What Marcus found strange was that he felt something needed to be said, but realized he had never really had this close a relationship with Tom. Before his brain had fully engaged, the words slipped out.

"You want a hug, big man?"

Tom's gaze dropped to the carpet, but his lopsided grin was almost comical. "Why? Do I look as though I need one?"

"No, it's just—Shit, I don't know why I said that." Marcus reddened at his own comment, feeling awkward.

"Appreciate the offer. But I'm good, thanks."

He met Tom's eyes, and they both chuckled and then fell quiet again.

"Listen, Tom," said Marcus quietly but with total conviction, "I promise you—*I promise*—that things are going to get better from now on."

Once again Tom's gaze dropped to the floor, but he gently nodded. Wanting to spare Tom any more embarrassment, Marcus opened the front door and stepped out into the night. A few strides down the path, before Tom had shut the door on him, he turned back.

"One last thing."

Standing there, he waited until he had Tom's full attention.

"Next time I come, I'm going to sit you down and, over a beer or two, explain to you exactly why the soccer team you support is such a large pile of dog poop. I mean, come on, really? They spend millions on new players and then come fourth in the league. Both coach and manager should be fired, and preferably from a cannon."

"Sod off, Vine."

But the wide grin on Tom's face was priceless.

Yes, thought Marcus, we can do this. Side by side we can put things back together again, maybe not the same as before, but at least help to bring some much-needed love and support back to the family.

On the way to his car, he didn't even realize he was whistling until a passerby—a woman walking her dog—smiled amiably at him.

Chapter Four

MONDAY morning Marcus parked along the road from Tom's house and checked the state of his hair, then his eyes, in the rearview mirror. Considering the exhausting weekend that had just been, he looked remarkably awake and alert.

End of April, and both Thursday and Friday lunch and dinner service had been off-the-scale busy. Then late Saturday night in Edgware Road, they had entertained a table of A-list celebrities—well, three, to be precise, all well-known personalities performing together in a West End show—and a group of other cast members. Marcus always welcomed celebs, purposely came out of his kitchen to meet them, and usually comped them a round of drinks. Other patrons enjoyed the display, and word usually got out either through the press or by word of mouth. And, of course, Tina loved free publicity.

On the downside, the revelers didn't leave until five thirty. Eventually, he got home from the restaurant just after midday, deciding to stay behind and finish the inventory, rather than coming back on Sunday afternoon. Now here he sat in his car, trying to come down to earth, readying himself for his domestic duties with the Bradford clan. Having woken at six that morning, he'd just about managed to get everything done and reach Tom's house by seven.

Talk about burning the candle at both ends.

"See you're in the paper again, Marcus," called Tom as soon as Marcus unlocked the front door using the set of keys Tom had cut for him. In the process of leaning over and packing documents into a briefcase, Tom gave Marcus a good view of his perfect jeans-clad backside, and despite his low energy, Marcus felt his cock stir. Absently, Tom waved a hand to the table where the girls were eating cereal.

"You're looking dapper this morning," said Marcus. As soon as the words were out of his mouth, he bit his tongue, remembering that Tom didn't like other men complimenting him. On anything. But this time the observation appeared to go right over his head. Usually when Tom worked on-site he donned worn overalls and a sweatshirt. Today he was togged out in clean jeans, a charcoal gray woolen jacket, a crisp white shirt, and a navy tie.

"Yeah, I know," muttered Tom, frowning at his attire. "Got a bloody boardroom meeting. Monday morning, of all things. The newspaper with the article's over on the table."

As far as Marcus was concerned, Tom needed to have more bloody boardroom meetings. Not that he didn't admire Tom in his trademark work clothes, but the casual corporate style definitely looked hot on the man.

"Daddy read it out to us," gurgled Charlotte, rewarding Marcus with the sight of a mouthful of milk and Cocoa Puffs.

"Charlie, what did Daddy say about eating and talking at the same time?"

"And close your mouth when you eat," added Katie. "Nobody needs to know what's in there. Nana said watching you eat is like looking at a washing machine running with a full load."

Marcus couldn't help but laugh aloud, while Tom smiled into his briefcase and gently shook his head. Fortunately Tom didn't notice the Cocoa Puff–covered tongue that poked out from Charlotte's mouth, aimed at her sister.

"I've left the page open at the article," said Tom before disappearing upstairs.

Marcus loved the early-morning routine with Tom and the girls, so different from the usual solitude of his own apartment. Six weeks since they'd had the chat, and everything already felt so much better.

More importantly, the social worker had turned out to be extremely understanding and sympathetic to Tom's situation. Having insisted on being there throughout the interview, Moira had given Marcus the full download. Tom, for his part, had been relieved they would not be considering further action, although the social worker confirmed that there would be monthly visits for the foreseeable future to ensure everything stayed on track.

Joining his goddaughters, Marcus parked himself on the free seat around the table and pulled the paper over. That morning he'd had barely enough time to get showered and dressed and make pack lunches for the family. Strange, too, because normally Tina would have called him. She scoured the national dailies each morning over breakfast, keen to capitalize on any publicity. When he picked up the paper, he realized why. This was a local rag, a freebie popped into everyone's letter box in Tom's borough. But the story was priceless.

Marcus vaguely remembered the situation. Apparently two of the paper's staff had rocked up at his Edgware Road branch one Thursday night—a traditionally busy night when Marcus usually ruled the kitchen—with a party of twelve, only to realize that nobody had made a booking. The head waiter—who would have been Michelle that night—had apologized that they wouldn't be able to fit them in, but then immediately phoned the Shepherd's Bush outlet and managed to secure them a table. Not only that, but she organized cabs for them all to be ferried across. The article, which took up a good half a page, then went on to talk up the excellent food and service, and was nothing short of solid gold publicity for Old Country. And of course, next to a photo of the outside of the Edgware Road restaurant was Marcus's standard publicity photo in his kitchen whites, holding a flour-peppered rolling pin and grinning at the camera.

"Right" came Tom's voice from behind, a heavy hand on Marcus's shoulder, which took Marcus by surprise, especially at how nice it felt there. "I need to be off. Final meeting today, but I think we're going to win this tender on the new estate in Burleigh. Finally a bit of good news."

"Excellent stuff. Go knock 'em dead."

"Thanks, honey," said Tom, squeezing Marcus's shoulder. "Uh, I mean Marcus."

For some reason the comment warmed Marcus inside, while Charlotte found this hilarious. After a few seconds almost choking and then the next tipping her head back in uncontrollable laughter with a tiny hand over her mouth, she finally managed to speak.

"Daddy just called Uncle Marcus *honey*."

Even Katie had trouble suppressing a fit of giggles. A smiling Tom came around the table and, from behind, kissed the top of Charlotte's head, then pulled her into his arms and rubbed his stubble into her cheek until she squealed even louder.

"That's what he used to say to Mummy," Katie explained, smiling still.

Yes, thought Marcus, they'd all come a long way if they could remember Raine without getting sad. While they had a family moment, Marcus stood and began clearing away bowls and packets of cereal from the table.

"I've made pack lunches," called Marcus to Tom from the open kitchen. "So no need for lunch money today. There's even one here for you, just in case."

"Remember Katie's got a checkup at ten. Her appointment card's on the table. Doctor's surgery is a stone's throw from here. Moira let Miss Colbert know she'll be in school just before lunch break."

"No problem. I'll swing by to pick up some groceries and then get the girls at the usual time. What do you fancy for dinner, ladies?"

"Shepherd's pie," shouted Charlotte, her all-time favorite.

"You always want shepherd's pie," said Katie. "We had it on Friday. Let Uncle Marc make something else for a change."

"I agree with Katie. Whatever you fancy cooking. God, you're a lucky so-and-so having Sundays and Mondays off," said Tom, picking up his case.

"Lucky?" replied Marcus, stopping halfway to the sink. "Do you know what time we finished on Saturday night? Sorry, scratch that, Sunday morning?"

"I know, I know. I'm sorry. You work hard when you're there. I am not disputing that. Just surprised you guys don't capitalize on the Sunday trade."

Many times Tina had tried to convince Marcus to open on Sunday, even if only for a lunch service to entice tourists to London. But after consulting many of his contemporaries in the trade, Marcus had stuck to his guns and decided to remain closed. His staff got one day off a week anyway, but the guarantee of Sunday with their families and loved ones definitely worked in his favor. Besides, he didn't need his accountant to tell him they were making healthy profits; the reservation lists for the next six months alone bore that out.

"If my manager has her way, we may well do. But for now things are going well enough that it's not a consideration. And anyway, I might have been otherwise engaged."

At that comment, Tom looked up from the letter he had scanned but not opened. "Oh, yes? And were you?"

"Might have been," said Marcus, flashing a wink at Tom. "Come on, Charlie, go brush your teeth and then Katie and I can drop you off to school."

He thought Tom might reward him with a knowing smile in return, but the man turned away and busied himself with his briefcase. Too much information, perhaps. Marcus made a mental note to keep his private life off-limits in conversation with Tom.

LATER that morning, after Marcus had dropped Charlotte off and returned home, as Katie packed her schoolbag while Marcus sat at the kitchen table organizing his accounts, the phone began to ring.

"Uncle Marc," said Katie, holding the phone out to Marcus. Her sad eyes said everything. "Someone's asking to speak to Mummy or Daddy."

Marcus hesitated. His heart stalled for a moment. Looking momentarily into Katie's gaze, he realized he had not been prepared for this. Nevertheless, he took the phone from her and placed the receiver to his ear.

"Hello?" he said tentatively.

"Good morning. I'm calling from Modern Dance Fitness" came a female voice attempting professionalism. His own trepidation evaporated in that haughtiness. "We're offering special memberships for people in your area. Sign up now for a three-year membership with nothing to pay for three months and then the option to renew on the same monthly terms."

"Thank you, but we're really not interested."

"This may be something more appropriate for Mrs. Bradford. Is she there, by the way, your wife? May I speak to her?"

Marcus found this kind of attitude in his restaurants irritating at the very least. The danger and, frankly, rudeness of making assumptions about a person based on gender alone was something he drilled into his waitstaff. He hated nothing worse than people assuming Raine was his wife when they were out together. Fortunately he knew how to deal with these people.

"Can I have your name, please?"

"I'm Debra Lingham."

"Debra. Can I ask you a question?"

"Yes, of course."

"Are you married?"

"Yes, I am."

"To a man?"

"Of course, to a man. What an odd question."

Another assumption, maybe even a touch of discrimination there. Hopefully he would never have to meet Debra Lingham in the flesh, because he might be tempted to give her a piece of his mind.

"Well, Debra. First of all, I'm a family friend, and today I'm the house sitter. Secondly, I really don't appreciate your telephone manner. If I tell you that we're not interested, then I speak for everyone."

"And I, Mr. Bradford, or whoever you are, am only doing my job. This happens to be an extremely generous offer, and you should consider yourself lucky that we are—"

Marcus slammed the phone down before the woman could say another word. Anger smoldered inside him. On top of everything else, had poor Tom had to put up with this kind of shit? When he turned and looked down, Katie stood there beaming at him.

"You sound just like Mummy sometimes," she said.

"Something you should know, Katie. Just because people are grown-ups doesn't mean they know how to be civil to other people. Some think they have the right to be rude just because of the job they do. My mother once told me that before I ever say anything to anybody which might be considered upsetting, I should think first of all how I would feel if someone said the same thing to me. Put myself in their shoes, so to speak. Your mummy was brilliant at doing that, which is why so many people liked her. One of her favorite sayings was 'courtesy costs nothing.'"

"What's courtesy?"

"It's politeness in a person's attitude or behavior. Your mummy was like that with everybody. Now, where's your appointment card?"

"It's in my bag. I'll probably need another prescription. Doctor said last time that if the asthma doesn't start to improve soon, he might consider other treatment. But at the moment I have to keep a diary of when I get attacks and rate them on a scale of one to five on how bad they are. There's a boy at school, Stephen, who uses a machine at home where he has to breathe in steam mixed with medicines for half an hour. But he doesn't mind because it's usually when the cartoons are on."

"Sometimes asthma just goes away with age, Katie," said Marcus, trying to sound encouraging. Growing up, Marcus's next-door neighbor and best friend had regular bouts of asthma that suddenly stopped when he hit puberty. Maybe some people were just lucky. On many a charity hospital visit, he'd met kids with far more serious medical conditions, but it just seemed unfair for someone so young to have to struggle with breathing when she should be outside enjoying the world.

Seven years old, thought Marcus, and already so much on her shoulders. There was absolutely no way he would ever walk away from this family again.

Chapter Five

A MONTH later, after another late finish at the Shepherd's Bush Old Country restaurant—this time a raucous hen party had kept them busy until after two in the morning—Marcus had happily headed home alone, asleep as soon as his head hit the pillow. Even as he went under, he resolved to have a slow, relaxed Sunday, which would entail a long snooze-in.

No such luck.

When the mobile phone went off on the bedside cabinet at eight, he was in two minds whether to let the call go to voicemail. Until he reluctantly cracked open his eyes and saw Tom's home number on the display.

"'Lo?" he croaked.

"Uncle Marc, Uncle Marc," shrieked Charlotte's excited voice down the phone. Marcus yanked the device away from his ear. "It's a sunny Sunday. And Daddy said if it was sunny today we could go to Water Kingdom. They have a Mayday special. But you have to come too. Katie needs to stay out of the sun. But if you come, I can go in the water with you and Daddy can stay with Katie."

In the background he could hear Tom telling Charlie to give him the phone.

"Melanie at school says they have a new waterslide for us small kids. But you have to be companied by an adult. So can you come, Uncle Marc? Pleeeease?"

Once again Tom's voice sounded in the background.

"Charlie, give me the phone. And will you please pipe down while Daddy talks to Uncle Marc?"

"Marcus" came Tom's warm voice as Charlotte continued to call out to Marcus. "Really sorry about that. She speed-dialed before I had a chance to stop her, the little madam. Listen, you don't have to do this. I imagine you had a late one last night, it being Saturday and the end of the month. And I know you like to sleep in Sundays. There'll be other days—"

"Give me an hour. To get ready and get over there."

"Are you sure?"

"Yeah," said Marcus, scrubbing a hand over his eyes before resting his forehead on his pale forearm. "Why not? Need an excuse to get moving on a Sunday. And to be honest, I could do with a dose of sunshine."

AFTER negotiating the long queue of excited families— seemed as though the whole world had the same idea that glorious Sunday morning—they finally made their way into the theme park. Tom led the girls away into a single-family cubicle while Marcus changed in the communal men's area. Apart from feeling a little tired, he felt grateful to be able to spend time with his surrogate family in the sunshine and also to road-test the skimpy designer swimmers his staff had bought him for Christmas. Comprised of comic superheroes in vibrant colors, the stretch material just about covered all the bases. After that, he spent a few minutes plastering on a reasonably protective UV factor sun lotion before donning his designer sunglasses and leather sandals. Unsurprisingly, he was ready and waiting a good ten minutes before Tom and the girls finally emerged. Leaning by a tree opposite the changing facilities, rucksack and cooler box at his feet, and safe behind his shades, he enjoyed noticing the passing stares of appraisal of both men and women.

Tom, by contrast—when they finally emerged— had stripped down to knee-length swimming shorts of navy blue cotton that might have been unflattering on anyone else. Fortunately he chose to go bare-chested, so at least Marcus, along with the rest of the water park, had the pleasure of seeing his defined arms and chest, complete with the mat of dark chest hair. Unlike Marcus, nothing about him had been gym-wrought, everything courtesy of his outdoor physical occupation. Shame he didn't feel the need to flaunt what he had. Maybe Marcus could work on that.

As soon as the two of them were near enough, both spoke the same words at exactly the same time.

"What the hell are you wearing?"

"Me?" said Tom before Marcus had a chance to reply. If Marcus was not mistaken, his cheeks had colored slightly. "*Indecent* doesn't even begin to describe those—panties. You're practically naked. Up close I can almost tell what religion you are."

"Ha, ha, very funny. At least I don't look like a 1950s soccer player. Exactly how old are those shorts?"

"I'll have you know these are Fred Perry's."

"Then I suggest you give them back to him."

"Yay, Uncle Marcus. Batman and Superman," said Charlotte, pointing to Marcus's swimwear. "And Wonder Woman. Yay. Daddy, you should get some."

"They're really cool, Uncle Marc," agreed Katie.

Marcus lowered his shades to gloat at Tom, which, in return, had Tom grinning and shaking his head.

"I think my point has been made, Grandpa. Now let's go and find somewhere to set up camp."

Although Water Kingdom was far from the largest water park in the country, the owners had created an open-air space where families could sit under real trees or on sun beds beneath parasols within easy viewing distance of their brood. More integrated parks had usually opted to house their slides under a large domed roof due to the unreliability of English summers. Water Kingdom sat open to the heavens, with only four towering twisty slides in blues and grays. In a smaller, shallower pool—Treasure Island Cove—they also catered to the smaller children, with shorter slides set amid plastic bamboo shoots and built into waterfalls, sliding down from pirate galleons or carved into models of giant fallen coconut trees.

Even Katie appeared to let go, splashing around in the water, always with her father close by her side. While Charlotte insisted on repeatedly riding the coconut slide with Marcus, after an hour Tom and Katie retreated to the dry shade of the tree where, earlier on, they had claimed a spot and made camp.

"I didn't want us to overdo it, otherwise Katie gets short of breath," said Tom, tossing Marcus's towel to him as they joined them forty-five minutes later.

"Totally understand," said Marcus, toweling himself down before doing the same to a giggling Charlotte. Once they had finished—the towel draped around his shoulders—and everyone settled, Marcus reached into his rucksack and pulled out some folded-up tartan material.

"Okay. Hands up if you're hungry?" he said. Of course both girls stuck their hands in the air.

"Because Uncle Marcus has brought a picnic. Charlie and Katie, you're in charge of the picnic blanket."

"Marcus, you didn't need to do that. I was going to take them to the park café."

"For junk food? Come on, Tom. You know me better than that. Most of this I already had in the fridge. The rest I brought home from the restaurant last night, rather than throw it away," he said, pulling plastic tubs, plates, and cutlery from his cooler. "Which includes, Mr. Bradford, our very own twist on someone's favorite dessert cake."

"You did not bring carrot cake?" said Tom, his eyes lighting up.

"Old Country carrot cake, indeed."

Later on, with everyone full, Marcus lay on his front in the sun. Tom took the girls to wash the plates and cutlery, and when they returned, they settled back in the shade. Marcus gave the girls one last task: to dispose of the litter in the three recycle bins opposite where they were sitting. He watched them go, holding the shopping bag full of litter between them.

"You're a real star for doing this," said Tom. "I hope you realize how much this means to them. And to me."

"My pleasure," said Marcus, turning to grin at Tom.

"They think the world of you, you know. Charlie's always asking me when you're coming over. Even Katie's doing so much better at school with your help. And don't you dare tell her, but that spread was better than anything Mum has ever cobbled together."

"All I need is a vagina and I could be your next girlfriend."

Tom went quiet at that remark, and Marcus instantly regretted the words. "Shit. Sorry, Tom. You know I have a smart mouth sometimes, don't you?"

"No," said Tom sadly, shaking his head. "It's not that. Mum's been on at me to start dating again. She thinks it's time. Says it couldn't do us any harm to have a little lady around. Someone to help ground the girls, someone on my arm when I'm doing work socials with other couples, that kind of stuff. I just can't get my head around the idea."

At that, Marcus sat up.

At first Tom's words had him irritated—at Moira's pushiness, at her insensitivity. Straight on the emotional heels followed a flash of anger quickly replaced by anxiety. Would Tom still need him if he had a new woman in his life? But then Tom had sounded unsure, hadn't he?

"Then don't. You'll know when the time's right. Get used to having things back on an even keel before you take the next step. Don't let anybody push you into doing anything you're not ready for."

Both men fell silent, watching the girls across the way as they hesitated before deciding which item of litter went into which recycle bin.

"Can I tell you something?" said Marcus, without turning.

"Go on."

"If I saw you with another woman right now, I'm not sure how I'd feel. Redundant, maybe. Because our combined efforts are finally paying off, and we're getting everything back on track. And I'm really enjoying being a part of the family again. Shit, does that make me a bad friend?"

"No, of course not," said Tom, and when Marcus finally turned around, he noticed Tom smiling his understanding. "I know what you mean. And it's great having you back."

EARLY in the afternoon, when Marcus returned from the park shop, bringing ice creams for Tom and Charlotte and an orange iced lolly for Katie, a woman togged out in a one-piece scarlet-with-black-polka-dots swimming suit complemented by an emerald green swimming cap came toward him. She looked like a human strawberry as she waddled away from Tom, waving over her shoulder. When she reached Marcus she stopped, leaned in, and squeezed his forearm. Turning to look back at Tom and the girls, she said one word.

"Adorable."

The moment Marcus followed her gaze, he smiled, knowing exactly what she meant. Tom sat with his back against the trunk of the oak, a proprietary arm around Katie. Lost in her new book, she sat leaning her back against him. On his other side, Charlotte, as hyperactive as ever, twirled around and around like a ballerina, hands clasped together above her head. Tom watched on, smiling, and leaned in to catch her when she inevitably fell over in a fit of giggles.

"Beautiful family."

"Yeah."

"You're very lucky."

"Yes, I suppose I am."

"You are," she said, moving beside him. Standing there briefly, she produced a wave that Charlotte returned enthusiastically. "You should be very proud. My son and his partner are talking about adopting. They live in Toronto. But they're a little nervous about what effect being brought up by two dads might have on the kid. Wish I could magic them over here right now to look at this happy little scene. That would make up their minds in a heartbeat."

Before Marcus fully caught on to her meaning and could correct her, she shuffled off. Had she thought Tom and he were a gay couple? They did get along pretty well together, so perhaps she could be forgiven for the assumption. Moving forward again, he wondered if he should say anything to Tom or if the remark might go down badly. No, best say nothing, he decided.

WHILE Tom looked after the girls, Marcus took the opportunity to try out one of the high curly slides. Nobody appeared to be able to pull off a dignified landing, most ending in an untidy mess of spray, limbs, and tangled swimming costumes. Even Marcus had to adjust his swimwear in the shallow waters before exiting the pool.

Letting the sun dry his skin, he took the opportunity to check out some of the men in the park. Most— married with wife and kids in tow—had let themselves go, but a few stood out. Even then, some of those in better shape were far too young for Marcus. In his honest opinion, the best-looking in-shape guy he had spied all day had arrived with him and sat now beneath the tree, reading Katie's book to her. As if hearing his thoughts, Tom looked up, then smiled and waved at Marcus. Typical, he thought, waving back. The one man he fancied had to be straight, someone he would never get to have. At some point, like Tom, he needed to get out there more and start seeing people. Or at least have another fling. Maybe he should bite the bullet and give Fereddique a call.

"Chef Vine" came a vaguely familiar voice to his left. "Gorgeous as ever."

Marcus turned to see a blond-haired Adonis approach him.

"Daniel? Dan Mosborough?"

Once upon a lifetime, Daniel Mosborough and Marcus had gone to the same high school. Although they had never been friends—Marcus was too tied up with Raine to bother spending much time with anyone else—both had sensed the other's difference from other boys in their class, or to be more precise, similarity to each other. When Marcus had bumped into Daniel in a popular gay club in Central London, neither had been surprised. Back then Daniel had been in demand. Slim and in the bloom of youth, he'd had men of all ages fawning over him.

Over time he had filled out. Gym-toned, he had clearly come over to flirt. Marcus had never really been into blonds, but Daniel was more a dirty blond— in every sense of the word if rumors were true—and even though his well-defined chest and thick muscled arms were naturally hairless, his thin tanned legs—a shortcoming of some of his gay gym-bunny friends— boasted a pelt of golden hair. Marcus could see that Daniel rarely worked his legs, so the overmuscled upper body appeared at odds with the spindly legs. Still, Marcus enjoyed the attention.

"What are you up to these days?"

"Just back from holiday. As you can probably tell," said Daniel, holding his hands out from each side of his waist as if to present the evidence. "Lanzarote with friends. Back to work Monday."

"And what is it you do now?"

"Still with the Met. Promoted to sergeant last September. Working out of Bromley Police Station."

"Wow. Well done, Dan."

"Me? What about you, Master Chef? Been watching you rise through the ranks with great interest. Me and a few of the boys from the station went to your place on Edgware Road. Asked if you were there that night. The girl on duty said you were working at the other restaurant. But everyone loved the food. Maybe one day you'll cook breakfast for me."

Yes, thought Marcus, still the same old Daniel.

"Maybe. If you play your cards right."

"Seriously, though, Marcus, you want to grab a drink sometime?"

Marcus had forgotten the incredible blue of Daniel's eyes. Had they not been to school together, he might have thought the man wore colored contacts. But no, Daniel had been blessed with amazing looks. And he was a copper now, so no doubt his wild days were behind him.

"Absolutely. Let me go get my mobile phone and get your number."

"Where are you sitting? I'll come over to you."

When Marcus pointed to Tom and the girls, Daniel turned to him, a confused expression on his face. "Sorry, mate. I thought you were still single."

"I am. That's Raine Fowler's husband and kids," said Marcus, and the instant pained expression that crossed Daniel's face told him that he need not say any more.

"Bloody terrible tragedy. The poor sods. My colleague was the first on the scene the day it happened. Absolute carnage," said Daniel, looking over at them briefly before bringing his attention back to Marcus. "And you've stayed connected?"

"I'm the girls' godfather. What else am I going to do?"

At that, Daniel folded his large arms and appraised Marcus afresh. "You know, I always knew you were one of the good guys. You and Raine didn't have time for me in school, but I remember being jealous of you both, like you were joined at the hip. Everyone but me thought you were dating. Let's definitely grab a drink soon."

"Stay here a minute. I'll grab my phone."

Marcus headed back to his rucksack and yanked out his phone.

"Who's that?" asked Tom.

"An old friend."

"Is he your boyfriend?" asked Katie.

"Katie!" said her father.

"His legs are too skinny. He looks like a rooster," said Charlotte.

"Charlotte!" said Tom.

"He's just a friend," said Marcus, laughing and then winking at Tom. "For now, anyway."

WITH them all fastened into Tom's Ford Edge, they began the hour-long drive back to Tom's house. Marcus had parked his SUV there so that they could all drive to the park together. Ten minutes into the journey and both girls slept soundly in the back seat, Charlotte secured in her booster seat, Katie next to her. Tom handled the car with quiet competence, ever conscious of driving smoothly so as not to disturb his cherubs.

At first Tom and Marcus listened to a radio channel playing popular music—purposely kept at a low volume—until the news came on. Tom, clearly not a lover of political news, instantly changed channels. On the new channel, once the announcer had finished speaking, Marcus realized they had tuned into a chat show. Instantly Tom snapped the radio off.

"What was wrong with the agony aunt show?" asked Marcus. "Are there any channels you actually like?"

"I don't mind nonstop music channels. At least I can still think while I'm driving. Not a fan of news channels. And I can't stand those dial-in chat shows. What on earth possesses people to call in and share their private lives, their innermost secrets, with the rest of the world?"

"Maybe they find it cathartic. Maybe they have nobody else to talk to."

"Come on, Marcus. Listen to them. That last woman, for example, who was moaning that her husband doesn't listen to her, doesn't communicate or understand her. Has she actually spoken to him to tell him the problem as she sees it, instead of phoning in and publicly whinging across the airwaves? These people are way beyond pathetic."

"Maybe. But some people get desperate. Don't you think it's better they voice their concerns than internalize them?"

"Yes, to a professional, not to a bloody disc jockey pretending to be some kind of professional psychiatrist. And then have the rest of the listeners hearing all about your issues and giving their own bloody suggestions. It's the sickest form of entertainment there is. If you ever had a personal problem, would you dial into one of those things?"

Marcus had to think about that for a moment. "Point taken. Probably not."

They both fell silent then. Tom's reaction should not have surprised him. Raine always said Tom preferred to suffer in silence rather than to talk problems through.

"So what's this guy like?" asked Tom.

"Which—oh, Daniel? He's okay. Pretty fit, actually. We used to go to school together. He's a police sergeant in Bromley now."

"He's a copper?" said Tom, swinging around to stare at Marcus.

"Yes," said Marcus, chuckling. "Don't worry, he was off duty today. And it's okay to be gay and in law enforcement these days, Mr. Bradford."

"I didn't mean—" said Tom, an admission of guilt if ever there was one. "You'll make a nice couple. Both have no sense of decency where swimwear is concerned."

"You're just jealous, Grandpa. And mark my words. One of these days, I'm going to get you into a pair of Speedos. You'd rock them."

Beside him Tom snorted but said nothing.

"Did you see the woman who came over to talk to us?" asked Tom after a few minutes of silence. "While you were away getting ice creams?"

"Looked like a bell pepper on legs?"

"Actually she was really nice. Chatted with Katie and complimented Charlie on her dancing. Said we were like the British equivalent of a modern family, whatever that meant, and that we ought to be on the cover of something called *Attitude*. Do you know what that is?"

Marcus couldn't help the laughter that burst from him.

"What?" asked Tom, turning to look quizzically at Marcus before returning his concentration to driving.

"*Attitude* is a British gay lifestyle magazine. And when she mentioned modern family, I think she was referring to the American comedy series that features male gay parents and their adopted daughter."

"She thought I was gay?" said Tom, horrified.

"She thought we were a couple," chuckled Marcus.

"Oh, I see." Tom fell silent then, appearing to process what Marcus had said.

"Does that bother you?"

"Why should it?"

But they spent the next thirty minutes of the journey home in silence. Not that Marcus minded. The scent of Tom's distinctive deodorant or body spray—he had no idea which—drifted across the space. And with only the sound of the traffic to distract him, together with Tom's soothing driving technique, Marcus soon found himself drifting off to sleep.

Even now, looking back, he had no idea why he opened his eyes at the exact moment the back of a white van appeared from nowhere, broadsiding the passenger side of their car.

Chapter Six

ALL Marcus remembered was his natural instinct to lean away as the van hit the front passenger door and the screech of metal upon metal as the car spun around. Even so, the impact thrust him sideways, and he smacked his head against the doorframe, producing a searing pain around his neck as the airbags inflated, and he blacked out.

When he awoke in a hospital bed, the doctor appeared to be more bothered about checking for a concussion rather than the fractured collarbone, which was apparently far less serious than the associated pain. Once he was fully conscious, Marcus's only concern was about the other passengers in the car.

"Everyone's fine," reassured Dr. Kimura, a tiny but clearly capable woman. "Fortunately the other driver was not traveling at great speed. The children don't even appear to have been shaken up—both were sleeping at the time."

"What about my friend Tom?"

"Absolutely fine," she said, and then her expression turned a little reprimanding. "He had the foresight to call an ambulance when he realized you'd been hurt. He's in the waiting room now. The grandmother took the children home. But your friend won't leave until he gets to see you. Do you feel well enough?"

"Yes, of course," said Marcus.

Five minutes later they led an ashen-faced Tom into the hospital room. First he took in the bandage around Marcus's head before meeting his eyes.

"Marcus. Jesus, I am so sorry."

"Wasn't your fault. The other guy backed out without looking."

"I should have spotted him. Should have been more vigilant."

"Tom, stop trying to be a superhero. I'm fine."

"Honestly, Marcus. Exactly how bad is it?"

"Minor. Doctor says I'll have my left arm in a sling for a couple of weeks, minor fracture of the clavicle, but they're keeping me in overnight because of the bump on my head. How are the girls?"

"They're okay. Worried about you, naturally. Charlotte slept through the whole thing, can you believe? Katie was the one who realized you weren't moving. Put the fear of God into me. I can't lose—"

And in that instant Tom lost control. Marcus was caught off guard, but with his good arm, he pulled Tom's head down onto his shoulder.

"Hey, hey, Tom," he said into his friend's ear, trying hard not to breathe in the man's wonderful musk. For reassurance, he squeezed his arm around Tom and held him tight. "It's minor. And you're not going to lose me. I'll be out tomorrow, I promise. It's just one night."

Over Tom's shoulder, Marcus watched as the ward door opened, presenting none other than Daniel Mosborough, who sauntered in, togged out in Bermuda shorts and a white polo shirt, but then froze when he saw the scene before him.

"What the hell are you doing here?" asked Marcus. Tom straightened up then and turned to see whom Marcus had addressed.

"Nice way to greet a friend," said Daniel, offering his hand to Tom. "Dan Mosborough. Marcus and I went to school together."

"You're the cop at the water park," said Tom, shaking hands.

"Ah, so I've already been talked about, have I?"

"Tom was admiring our similar taste in swimwear," said Marcus, beginning to laugh again but then thinking better of it. "I thought you might be here in an official capacity. I'm just surprised you found out what happened so quickly."

"I was chatting to one of my team, who was passing the water park and offered me a lift home in his squad car. Stopped when we got to the scene. Then one of my boys mentioned your name and what had happened. I thought I'd head over here to check on you."

"Listen," said Tom, "I'll let you guys chat. I need to go and fetch the girls. See you tomorrow, Marcus. Call me if you need anything."

After they'd all said their farewells, Dan stayed behind and pulled up a chair. "He's a bit of a hunk."

"Hands off, Mosborough. He's straight."

"Oh yeah? I caught the two of you having a quick smooch."

"We were not bloody—shit," said Marcus, wincing. "Please don't make me laugh."

"Sorry, mate."

"So are you here to interrogate me?"

"Course not. From what I understand, there's not a lot to tell. Van driver—guy in his twenties, no previous—using his driver's side wing mirror, tried to avoid a car parked on his right and didn't see you until it was too late. Luckily Bradford wasn't driving fast, otherwise it might have been much worse."

"He's a bloody good driver. Honestly, Dan, all I remember is waking suddenly to see the back doors of the van hit. Then I blacked out."

"Yeah. Apparently Bradford told my colleague the same thing. You in much pain?"

"Doctor's got me on some expensive meds. Just waiting for them to kick in. But no doubt it'll hurt tomorrow."

"Dr. Kimura's more worried about him showing any signs of concussion, Sergeant," interrupted the staff nurse, coming to the end of the bed and checking a chart. "We're keeping him in overnight, just in case. If you start to feel dizzy or nauseous or if you have trouble with your vision, make sure you press that buzzer straightaway."

She disappeared as quickly as she'd turned up. A short pause fell between them.

"Good to meet you today, Dan. And now it'll definitely be memorable."

Marcus let Daniel chuckle without joining in.

"Hope you don't mind me sticking around?" said Dan, pulling up a chair. "I've got bugger all else to do. Not back on duty until tomorrow. But I'm having a pint with some of the lads later."

"Had it been my choice, I'd have preferred a chat over a pint too, but I suppose here's as good a place as any. So where shall we begin? Maybe you could go first. Anyone special in your life since school?"

Marcus couldn't be sure, but he thought he noticed a slight flicker of sadness cross Dan's face before he paused to consider.

"I did. Zane. Six years ago. Fellow copper, different unit. Unlike me, though, he wasn't out, so difficult doesn't even begin to explain our relationship. But let me tell you, it's tough being with someone who refuses to put even one foot out of the closet. Spent most of our time together either in his flat or mine, watching cable movies, eating takeout and drinking beers, followed by nights of pretty amazing sex. But being indoors all the time gets old fast. Wouldn't even entertain the idea of a movie night at the cinema in case he got spotted with me. Final straw came when we went to the other side of the planet on holiday together—San Francisco—and he wouldn't even let me touch him in public. No way to live a life."

"I'm really sorry."

Daniel shrugged, but the experience had clearly affected him. "Since then, nobody special. Threw myself into my career instead."

"You and me both. You ever see him? Zane?"

"Couple of times. Even though it was the right decision, you can't just turn off your heart. The couple of times we've run into each other—usually some official meeting or another—my stomach goes into a tailspin. So how about you? Anyone special?"

"Nah. An occasional roll in the hay, but no keepers."

"You and Tom Bradford seem pretty tight."

"Come off it, Dan," said Marcus, but Tom's instant of vulnerability earlier had confused him. "He's got enough on his plate right now. Taken on a whole lot of strife since Raine died."

"You fancy him, though, don't you? I can tell by the way you look at him."

"He's family. But I once told Raine that if he'd had a gay twin brother, I'd be the first in line."

Once again they both fell silent.

"Talking of Raine, you obviously remembered the crash that took her life."

"Difficult to forget."

"At the time, she was traveling with a man called Damian Stone."

"Is that so?"

"Yes. At first Tom thought she might have been having a fling with the guy. But that's not the case. They attended the same yoga class. But then they died on the M25, nowhere near the yoga school. I still keep asking myself why."

"Sometimes we don't really know those closest to us."

"You're not a fan of radio chat shows, are you?"

"Huh?"

"Sorry. In-joke between Tom and I. Yes, I've heard that people close to us can turn out to be a total mystery. But you know me, and I did know Raine. She would never do anything like that. She had too much to lose."

"But the mystery remains. What was she doing in the car with this guy?"

"Exactly. Tom said just let it go."

"Wise words. Nothing's going to bring her back."

"Yeah, Tom said that too."

"But you want me to look into it?"

"No, of course not," said Marcus firmly, before hesitantly continuing. "Unless. Could you? I mean, I wouldn't want to get you into any trouble."

"You wouldn't. To be honest, it'd be a doddle. There's bound to be a case file, probably on computer. Not as though it's a murder case or anything. But you'll owe me."

"And what exactly would I owe you?"

"Dinner?"

"I think I can manage that."

Just at that moment, Marcus's phone buzzed. Tina's face popped up on the display as he raised the device to his ear. He took a deep breath, wondering how he would explain his current predicament.

"And maybe a blow job."

"Yeah," replied Marcus, grinning. "Well, let's see what you come up with before I commit to any after-school activities."

Daniel had a nice laugh, and Marcus smiled as he answered the phone.

"Who's that laughing with you?" asked Tina. "Someone clearly in a good mood. Where are you?"

"In hospital. Being treated for concussion and a fractured collarbone."

"What! Are you being serious?"

Marcus took a few minutes to explain to Tina, who calmed significantly when he explained the less serious nature of the accident. What took a little longer was convincing her that she did not need to rush to see him.

"So what's up? Why are you calling on a Sunday?" said Marcus, trying to distract her from her mother hen routine.

"Well, I'd hoped it would be good news, but it depends on you now, and how quickly you're going to recover. Kurt Bruckmeyer's managed to get the New York deal back on track." Since their return, a couple of key investors had decided to back out despite Tina's efforts to convince them of Marcus's commitment to the project. "He's managed to drum up a batch of new investors, but he wants us to move fast. Apparently that celebrity chef program you featured on just aired in New York. But it means there'll be back-to-back meetings in three weeks' time. So, of course, they want to meet the star in person. Are you going to be okay?"

"Physically, yes. But am I going to have to shag Bruckmeyer just to prove good faith?"

Marcus had to look away from Dan's shocked expression to stop from laughing, but Tina's comeback caught him off guard.

"I think that ship has already sailed, sweetie."

"Ow," said Marcus. "How long are we going to be away for?"

"Hard to say, but I'd clear space for three weeks to be on the safe side."

The humor left Marcus then. Not only would he need to brief his staff to cope without him, but he'd need to reschedule things with Tom and Moira. When he ended the call with Tina, he noticed Dan still standing there.

"Anything I can do to help?" he asked.

"Yeah. Put the bloody sports channel on the TV and then bugger off and see your mates. At least one of us should be enjoying a night off, and it looks like I'm stuck here on my back for the night."

"Hey, keep smiling. Let me see what I can do to trace your man."

Even though he chose to live alone, once Daniel had gone, Marcus had never felt so abandoned in his whole life.

Chapter Seven

IF Marcus had to sit in one more New York oak-paneled boardroom, waiting for yet another self-important businessman who thought it perfectly acceptable to keep him waiting for more than half an hour, he was likely to throw one of the room's expensive leather and chrome chairs through the window. Not that doing so would help matters. Most of the floor-to-ceiling windows would likely be reinforced and unbreakable, and he would simply end up with a metal chair in the face, or worse still, a newly rebroken collarbone.

"Sorry 'bout this," said Kurt, glancing again at his special edition Rolex.

"For heaven's sake, chill out, Marcus" came Tina's stern voice. While Kurt had been nothing but charming and apologetic, Tina had been her usual reproving self.

"You've got a face like a samurai warrior's mask. The sooner you charm the pants off this man and get him on board, the quicker we can head out of here."

Tina had a point. He had been behaving petulantly. Only because three weeks away from home had turned into almost four. This last person—Kim Kendrick—had shown an interest right at the last knockings. Kurt hadn't even met him, but an enthusiastic email had persuaded Tina that one extra investor could do no harm. As usual, she was right, even though Kurt had stuck to his word and already managed to get a whole raft of influential businesspeople on board. In fact, everything appeared far too optimistic. Marcus had never really grasped the fact that the restaurant name, Old Country, could have such a nostalgic effect on people. Many of the American investors immediately wanted to tell him stories about their British heritage.

As for Kurt, he had turned out to be an absolute gem. Already familiar with the more exclusive restaurant trade in New York, he had recommended sites for the restaurant, knew the best wholesalers for kitchen equipment, and had already contacted a few talented chefs and kitchen staff to explore their interest in the venture and give them the heads-up in case they wanted in.

Best of all, Marcus would get to have the final say without having to be around to check every minor detail. With both Tina and Kurt in his corner, everyone had agreed that the basic setup choices would remain his—his intellectual property, so to speak—kitchen fit-out, branded restaurant design, full menu selection, staffing choices, and that he would only be needed for the initial launch for the sake of publicity. There would be no flying back and forth from London to New York like his regular jaunts between Edgware Road and

Shepherd's Bush. Of course, he was under no illusion
about the competition in New York. Some of the finest
chefs in the world had set up shop there. But market
research—again courtesy of Kurt—suggested that his
special spin on British food was likely to succeed. As
with everything, only time would tell.

Right then the large oak door to the boardroom
swung open.

Pushing a wheeled silver tray carrying white bone
china teacups, a matching pot of tea, and a cake stand
filled with an assortment of sandwiches and cakes was
one of the most handsome men Marcus had ever laid
eyes on. Kurt jumped to his feet and ran to hold the
door open, no doubt partly out of curiosity, partly out of
instant infatuation. Whoever the man was, he possessed
the kind of hypnotic blue-eyed gaze reserved for movie
stars or top models, one that could cause people to walk
into lampposts or trip off sidewalks—eyes a person
melted into.

Normally Marcus would have fought Kurt to be the first
one out of his seat, drooling over the man, but oddly enough,
even though his head understood the attractiveness—just as
he would acknowledge the beauty of a work of art—his
libido remained dormant. Interesting.

"Mr. Vine, Mr. Bruckmeyer, and Mrs. Adebayo-
Cruickshank. Believe it or not, I am a strong believer
that lateness is the worst kind of bad manners" came the
warm baritone. "But in my defense, my driver was stuck
behind a truck that decided to break down four blocks
from here. Otherwise the Earl Grey would have been
waiting for you. I'm Kim Kendrick, by the way."

Almost as soon as they got chatting, Marcus
realized what a good call they had made. Kim loved
the concept, his parents both of Scottish descent, and

more importantly, just like Kurt but mixing in different circles, Kim knew people. As they left with the new sponsor in their pocket, Marcus not only received a warm, firm handshake from the Adonis, but also got a grin and a wink. Did the man bat for their team?

Unfortunately, he still felt nothing. As they stood quietly in the elevator on the way down, he made a mental note to visit a doctor when he got back to England.

RAGGEDLY tired and sporting a nagging headache, he should have headed straight for home, but during the flight, he made up his mind to drop into the Bradford family gathering as soon as he landed that Sunday. Tina had stayed behind in New York to deal with dangling business matters, so he was truly flying solo. Besides that, he told himself, he had bought the girls presents from a couple of cute downtown toy stores, including a model-sized Staten Island Ferry for Katie—as explicitly instructed—so it made perfect sense to head straight there, rather than haul them all the way home. In reality, he craved familiar company and wanted to surprise them as well as experience a dose of the normalcy that being a part of the Bradford clan had returned to him.

And someone up there surely agreed, because originally he thought the late arrival time might mean the girls would already be tired from a day spent playing in the back garden. But with the benefit of a strong tailwind, the pilot made good time and they touched down almost bang on midday, forty minutes earlier than the scheduled arrival time. And such a glorious English day in mid-July too, verdant shades of patchwork fields showcased on either side of the plane as they approached Heathrow.

Even the airport—one of the busiest in the world—
appeared controlled and efficient as he passed seamlessly
through immigration, and then baggage claim, out to his
waiting cab driver. Some days things just worked.

An hour later, his car pulled up outside John and
Moira's pretty semidetached house of red brick and
pebble dash, the front garden boasting well-ordered
rosebushes of white, pink, and burgundy, and the
regimental verdant stripes of a neatly mown front
lawn—Moira's pride and joy. At the open car boot, he
paid the driver with a handsome tip—something Tina
would have actively discouraged—before hauling his
gift bags and pull-along luggage to the familiar front
door of oak with stained glass panels. After pressing
the doorbell a couple of times and hearing nothing, he
decided to try the knocker. Five minutes later, he was
about to head around the side of the house when the
door swung open.

"Still doesn't work" came Moira's prim voice.
"The bell, that is. Something else Tom says he's going
to fix. Although in which century, heaven only knows."

"Afternoon, Moira."

"Hello, dear," said Moira, leaning forward and
giving him a light peck on the cheek, so different to his
own parents, who were fierce huggers. "Tom will be
glad to see you. Been having kittens trying to balance
everything while you've been away. But for goodness'
sake, don't tell him I told you so."

"Wouldn't dream of it."

WHEN Marcus stepped through the kitchen door into
the back garden, Charlotte spotted him first and hurtled
over, screaming his name out loud. Everyone else

stopped talking and turned to look. So much for making a low-key entrance. Colliding into him, she wrapped her arms around his upper thigh. Bless her, Marcus could see she had a runny nose, most likely from a recent cold, and clutched a handkerchief in one hand. But even that couldn't dampen her spirits. Katie, ever the cool one, followed with far more dignity but couldn't resist the smile that tugged at her mouth. When Marcus knelt down, Charlotte fell into his arms and even Katie stepped forward for a tight hug.

"Missed you, Uncle Marcus," she whispered, and after kissing the top of her head, Marcus had to look elsewhere, his eyes stinging, in an effort to stop from choking up. Like her father, Katie rarely showed any emotion.

"I missed you too, princess. But I've brought prezzies."

Charlotte, of course, squealed then, jumping up and down before being stalled by a fit of coughing. Marcus put his bags down, then took the handkerchief from Charlotte and wiped her nose. Satisfied, and with Katie standing by patiently, Marcus handed one of the bags to her little sister. Of all people, Tina had been the one to discover the Cabbage Patch doll shop and suggested the colorful family collection for Charlotte. Katie knew what Marcus had bought her, but maybe for his benefit, she looked suitably surprised as she pulled the present from the bag. Very faintly, he could hear her wheezing—not enough to warrant using the inhaler— and guessed she had overexerted herself. With the two of them distracted, he took the opportunity to survey the rest of the garden.

Tom's father, John, sat in his wheelchair at the head of the wooden bench, surrounded on either side by people Marcus didn't recognize—two couples of a similar age to

Moira and John, neighbors probably. John, a quiet man who usually let his wife take the reins, always found time to chat with Marcus, treated him almost like a second son. In fact, he usually saved up little bits of sports trivia, knowing and approving of Marcus's favorite soccer team. In many ways, Tom was a lot like his father.

Alone on a tartan picnic rug beneath the apple tree amid a pile of children's books and toys, Tom lay on his side with his long jeans-clad legs stretched out and a fresh linen shirt open at the neck to reveal the beginnings of his chest hair. That, coupled with the heart-stopping smile on his face from watching his girls' excitement, made Marcus's heart speed up, that tremble of anticipation he got whenever he checked someone out. Except. Why hadn't that happened when he'd met Kim Kendrick?

Before he had a chance to berate himself, something about Tom changed. When his gaze met Marcus's, a fleeting transition occurred, his smile fading, his eyes reflecting sadness and then—what was that? Anger? What the hell was that all about? Maybe because Marcus had been away longer than planned. Marcus pasted on his best smile and held a palm up in greeting, mouthing the words "hey there." In return, Tom caught himself, shook his head almost imperceptibly, and raised his beer bottle in salute.

Once Marcus had unwrapped himself from the girls and did a quick once-around the people gathered, he sauntered over to Tom. Weighing down his jacket pocket was the last of his gifts, which he pulled out. A bottle of twenty-year-old Irish malt whiskey, Tom's favorite. Once Tom had managed a polite thanks, the two remained in silence together, Tom sitting, Marcus standing.

"Everything okay?" asked Marcus.

"Yeah, everything's—" Tom hesitated before sitting up straight, back against the tree trunk. "Yes. So how'd it go in doodle-dandy-land?"

"Touch-and-go for a few moments there. We managed to get most of the investors lined up, but two of the key players had last-minute scheduling problems. Which is why I'm back later than expected. But lucky for me, Tina managed to get everything pulled back on track in the last couple of days."

Marcus didn't notice at first because he had been scanning the garden, but Tom had gone silent again. When he peered down, he found Tom staring up intently at him, and he didn't appear to have been listening. "You sure you're okay, mate?"

"Yeah," said Tom almost sheepishly, as though he had been caught doing something illicit. "It's just… really good to see you."

Marcus smiled broadly at that, the warmth of the remark filling his chest. Tom rarely let his guard down and even more rarely gave compliments to anyone. Marcus dropped down next to him, shuffled up, and bumped shoulders.

"You too," said Marcus, relaxing against the tree trunk. "And I'm truly sorry about the delay getting home. Everything back to normal tomorrow. I'll pick the girls up first thing."

"No, it wasn't—business has to come first. And we just about managed to survive. Although Mum was almost pulling her hair out. I just want you to know how much I—we all—value what you're doing for us."

"You're family now, Tom. Or as close as I'll ever get. Of course I'm going to be here for you. It's where I want to be."

This time Tom looked away, a hand smoothed briefly over his mouth.

"Yeah, well," he muttered. "Just needed saying."

Chapter Eight

DANIEL turning up at the Shepherd's Bush restaurant in uniform at the tail end of a busy Saturday lunchtime was an unexpected but not unpleasant surprise. In fact, he looked hotter in uniform than he did in white Speedos or Bermuda shorts. Benny, the front-of-house manager, had zeroed in on the policeman and, once he realized Daniel was there unofficially, flirted outrageously. If anyone could give Daniel a run for his money on the flirtatiousness stakes, Benny was the man. However, today Daniel was all business, strictly professional and only grinning good-naturedly and nodding at Benny's double entendres. Fortunately Benny gave everyone the same treatment—for most people the straight-faced delivery of his innuendos meant that many went over their heads—so he would have been blissfully unaware that Daniel batted for his team.

Between Marcus's stint in the hospital and his time in New York, they had called each other a couple of times trying to synchronize calendars for a night out. But through no fault of either, this had proven difficult, both having busy professions. Marcus often had to head into work at short notice to deal with one crisis or another, while Daniel was frequently called upon to work overtime.

But finally they'd managed to meet one Tuesday afternoon in late July for a drink in a small local bar on Marylebone High Street, a few blocks from the restaurant. Marcus had finished the lunchtime service at Edgware Road and Daniel, in jeans and a tee, had been on a training course in Hendon, dropped off by a colleague.

Daniel had drunk designer Belgium beer straight from the bottle, taking great pride in talking about the fermentation process, the history of the beer brewed by Trappist monks—clearly a veritable expert on the product. One particular brand, a strawberry-flavored lager with a reasonably high alcohol content, had been a favorite of his for many years. At the time, Marcus could think of nothing worse than strawberry-flavored beer, but had sampled some and made encouraging noises when offered out of sheer politeness.

The meeting had been cordial and almost formal, and Marcus had begun to realize nothing was ever going to happen between them, even before Daniel got called away within the hour after a brief but highly charged call from a colleague back at the station.

"You want something to eat?" asked Marcus, stepping out of the kitchen, wiping his forehead with a cloth as Benny sashayed off to see to another customer.

"Your man over there's a piece of work," said Daniel, nodding to the departing backside of Benny.

"But a bloody good and loyal worker. So to what do I owe this very nice pleasure?"

"Too early for that dinner you owe me, I suppose?"

Marcus tilted his head quizzically, not sure what Daniel meant.

"Is there somewhere we can sit, mate? I found out some things for you."

"Damian Stone?" said Marcus, looking up eagerly. "Come into the back office."

"Not a whole lot, I'm afraid," said Daniel when seated in the tiny storage room that doubled as an office. "Twenty-five-year-old single Caucasian male from Frenton, regional marketing manager for a high street bookstore chain, no previous convictions, total clean slate."

"Well, that settles that," said Marcus, arms folded.

"What?" asked Daniel, shaking his head, not understanding.

"She was into older men. Tom's ten years older. Still doesn't explain why she was in the car that Friday lunchtime."

"Off for a weekend romp, maybe?"

"No way. Anyway, she was supposed to attend a dinner party with Tom's work people that evening. That's why Moira picked up the girls from school."

"Thank goodness," said Daniel.

"But thanks for doing this, anyway, Daniel. Listen, I've been given complimentary tickets to a champagne brunch at a new hotel opening in the next couple of months. Sunday from eleven. Oysters, caviar, lobster, carvery, champers—the works. Thought it might be right up your street. How do you fancy being my date?"

"In lieu of dinner?"

"As well, if you like?"

"Sure. Let's do the brunch," he replied, grinning and slipping a piece of paper across the table. "More likely to work this time, if it's a Sunday."

"What's this?" asked Marcus.

"Stone's address. In case you wanted to make contact. Or if you could steal an hour or two off work right now, we could drive over there together."

DAMIAN Stone's house turned out to be a small but pretty Victorian terraced cottage bordering the common in Frenton. Snug, Raine would have called the place. Maybe she had, if they'd been friends. Walking up to the front door, he had a moment of trepidation. Daniel must have noticed, because he stepped forward to take the lead. Would the occupant be more or less likely to open up with a uniformed officer present? Marcus had no idea. Moreover, in the time since the accident, Stone's family may have already sold the house. Would the new occupants have any idea about the previous owner? At the very least they might be able to point Marcus in the direction of Stone's family. Or maybe Stone had a girlfriend who still lived here and might have known nothing about Lorraine being in the car. How awkward would that be?

While Marcus had been lost in thought, Daniel had already rung the doorbell. Pretty chimes echoed faintly from inside. As the silhouette of a figure filled the large frosted glass door panel, Daniel removed his cap.

"Can I help?" asked the man, opening the door wide before looking suspiciously at Daniel and taking in his uniform.

Slight of build, the man was not unattractive, but had a slight stoop forward, as though he had been hauling heavy weights around on his back all his life. If Marcus were to guess, he'd put the man in his early to midthirties. As the man was dressed a little shabbily in a soiled tee and jeans, Marcus assumed they had interrupted him doing some gardening or maybe home maintenance.

"Sergeant Mosborough. Kent Police. Are you the owner of this house?"

"I am now. Why? What's this about?"

"And your name is?"

"Ken. Kenneth Villers. If this is about the break-in at number fifteen, I told your lot already that I didn't see nothing. I was out all night with friends."

"This isn't about the break-in. It's about a previous occupant, Mr. Damian Stone. Can we come in for a moment?"

"Damian's dead," said the man, his voice quieting.

"Yes, we're aware of that. May we come in?"

Hearing Daniel slip into his official mode made Marcus grin. When the man held the door open obediently, Marcus followed in behind. The front door opened straight into a living area, with an old dark metal fireplace and grate, but now housing a gas version of a coal fire. With pine floorboards and bronze light fixtures, the old place had been beautifully renovated and decorated. Someone had very good taste. Either that or this guy had a lot more money than his appearance belied. Villers offered them a seat on a long brown leather chesterfield. Marcus sat, but Daniel remained standing.

"Mind if I use your bathroom, sir?" asked Daniel.

"Top of the stairs, on the right."

"Cup of tea would be nice," said Daniel, heading toward the stairs. "Milk with one sugar for me."

Despite a barely audible sigh, Ken stepped into the open kitchen—much like Tom's place but with more modern appliances—and began setting about filling a kettle with water.

While Marcus sat there, his phone beeped. When he pulled the phone out, the message from Tom read simply, *girls want to go to a small farm tomorrow and want Uncle Marc to come along, too. Interested?*

Marcus sighed. As well as sacrificing another Sunday morning, he would have to spend the day trying his best not to ogle Tom. He texted back a simple *count me in*.

"So why are you with the copper?" asked Villers.

"Look, I'm sorry about this, Ken. He's actually a friend helping me out. We're not here for any official reason. It's just that I knew the woman in the car who was with Damian and wondered if you might have some answers."

"Bradford? The one who died in the crash?"

"That's right. Lorraine. So he *had* mentioned her before?"

"Not sure. They may have done yoga together. Then again, Stoner talked a lot of names. S'what marketing people do, names and places, organizing events and book signings, making guest lists. I rarely listened."

"I see," said Marcus.

"You her husband?"

"No," said Marcus. "Her best friend."

Just then Daniel came down the stairs and entered the room, holding a large silver-framed photograph in his hands. After flashing the photo at Marcus, he held the picture in front of his chest. The picture had Ken and another man standing together smiling. Done up in matching white tuxedos and black bow ties, drinking champagne from crystal flutes, they stood together on grand stone steps—the photographer positioned a couple of steps below them—while in the background a row of Doric columns indicated some kind of official building, a museum perhaps.

"That's private property," said Villers, stopping what he was doing.

"How long were you and Mr. Stone married?" asked Daniel.

What the hell? Marcus's jaw dropped at that. But then, when he studied the photograph again, the fact was so blatant. Each held a glass out, but the fingers of each other's hands were entwined in the other's. Maybe you could call Damian Stone attractive, but not in a masculine sense. If Marcus had to use a word to describe him, he would have used the word pretty. In the picture, he appeared to be wearing eyeliner.

"Not married. Civil partnership. Three years," said Ken.

"Oh God, Ken. I'm so sorry," said Marcus.

"Yeah, well. Shit happens. Had over a year to try to get used to it," said Ken, dropping tea bags into mugs and keeping his head down. But Marcus could hear in his voice that the memory still hurt. When Ken brought mugs of tea over and placed one on a coaster in front of Marcus, he paused a moment, looking puzzled into Marcus's eyes.

"I know you, don't I?"

For a moment, Marcus felt a rush of optimism. Had he met Ken and Damian Stone before while with Raine? And if so, when?

"Yeah," said Ken, handing another mug to Daniel but with his gaze still on Marcus. "You're that chef on the telly. Vine. The one what does traditional British food. Me and Stoner had our anniversary dinner at your Shepherd's Bush restaurant. Your head waiter was a star. Made us feel really special. You're one of us too, ain't you?"

"I am. And I'm really pleased we gave you a good memory."

"Were you and Mr. Stone exclusive?" asked Daniel out of the blue. While Marcus and Ken sat, Daniel remained standing by a bookcase. Marcus couldn't help but show his disgust at the question, but Ken didn't appear to mind.

"Mostly, yeah. We had an understanding."

"What kind of an understanding? Did Mr. Stone date women too?"

"Dan!" said Marcus.

Ken's sudden laugh sounded like someone sawing wood. "Damian used to tell people he was a prototype gay, a solid six on the Kinsey scale. He was one of those blokes who you just know are gay as soon as they open their mouths. The girls at work loved him like the brother they never had; they all turned out for his funeral. But if a woman ever hit on him, he'd run a mile screaming. And to be fair to him, Stoner wasn't the one of us who messed around. Most of the time he was too busy. Either fixing up this place—he was the designer and decorator—or doing his jobs. But I had urges every now and then. He understood that."

"So," said Marcus to Daniel, "that answers that mystery. Raine was definitely not having an affair with Damian."

But Daniel had already moved on. "Did you know where he was heading the Friday they died?"

"No. He did yoga in the morning and should have been home that afternoon."

"At the Cumberland Health Sanctuary?"

"That's the one."

"Still doesn't answer what they were doing driving south on the M25," said Daniel.

"Look," said Ken, "I don't know if this helps, but sometimes Stoner did a bit of moonlighting. His company would have fired his arse if they'd known. But I'd sometimes help out if they were shorthanded."

"What kind of moonlighting?" asked Daniel in full interrogation mode.

"Organizing kids' parties, weddings, anniversaries, that kind of thing. He'd sort out venues, catering, staff, invitations, and everything. Reckoned that once he'd saved up enough, he was going to set up a full-time business. Get away from those bloodsucking corporate bastards."

At first Marcus couldn't see how that information helped, but once again Daniel piped up. "Did he have a list of preferred venues?"

"He did, as it goes. Five or six. Mainly around London. Usually depended on where the client lived or whether the guests needed accommodation too."

"Any chance we can have a look?"

This time Ken simply reached around Daniel to a large box folder in the bookcase. He proffered the file to Daniel. "Knock yourself out."

Marcus was not sure exactly what Daniel expected to find, but rather than question him, he went along with the idea. Daniel had the professional experience, after all. Forty-five minutes later, they came up with invoices from six venues Damian had used over the past three years, all dotted around the home counties and within easy reach of the M25.

"What exactly are we looking for, Dan?"

"It's just a theory," he said, jotting down contact details in his notepad from each of the invoices. "But maybe Raine was organizing an event. Maybe something for the kids. Who better to help with the arrangements than her gay yoga buddy?"

"Me, Dan. I'm her best gay buddy. If Raine had been organizing an event and wanted professional help, she would have come to me."

"Point taken. Then maybe Raine was assisting Damian with an event. What did you say she did for a living?"

"I didn't. But she worked part-time in a local naturopathic store. Selling and advising on alternative medicines, vitamins, herbs. That kind of thing."

"She ever do any work in your restaurant? Wait tables or serve drinks?"

"Not a chance in hell. Raine, for all her positive traits, was naturally uncoordinated where restaurant or kitchen work was concerned. The only position she'd have suited brilliantly would have been the maître d's role: meet, greet, and seat guests. But I already had those roles filled. And it's not a job a caterer needs."

"Still, it can't do any harm giving these numbers a ring and checking if they remember having had any bookings from Stone or Bradford. Leave that with me and I'll call you if I find anything."

On their way out, Daniel thanked Ken for being so helpful and compliant, but Marcus stopped at the door and pulled out something from his wallet.

"Look, Ken. I know how hard it is to lose someone you care for. And this doesn't really go anywhere near to helping fill that hole. But if you do find yourself uptown with a friend and fancy a free meal at Old Country—anything you want, my treat—just show this card to the head waiter. Or give me a call beforehand and I'll make sure we reserve a table for you."

"Wow," said Ken, clearly taken aback. "That's really… that's really nice. Thanks, Marcus. One last favor?"

"Go on."

"Any chance of a selfie with you? Otherwise my mates will never believe you were here in my home."

Daniel patiently took the photos on Ken's phone, shaking his head and smiling. But even he seemed pleased with Marcus as he drove him back to the restaurant.

Chapter Nine

SOMETHING was up.

All day Marcus had gone out of his way to be cordial and civil to Tom. Overnight he had made a conscious decision to manage his emotions around the man. Nothing overfriendly, simply nodding in all the right places and answering questions and making sure his topics of conversation centered mainly around the girls. But Tom had barely spoken to him or made eye contact the whole day. Eventually, after asking twice if Tom was okay and getting a curt "fine" in response, he gave up trying and concentrated on keeping the girls entertained.

When Marcus first reached their house that dreary Sunday, he had walked in on Charlotte insisting they "go and see Mummy" before heading to the farm. Privately Marcus had been pleased to have been included in the family ceremony. As usual, they'd taken Tom's car and had driven to the cemetery together. Initially Marcus had ascribed Tom's moodiness to the somber ritual. He'd ached to tell Tom what he'd learned about Damian Stone, but he had never found the right time. Then, while Tom and Charlotte went to pick wildflowers together, Marcus had stayed under his huge umbrella with Katie.

Once they were on their way, apart from the awful weather—Sunday had brought the kind of light but nagging rain that fell constantly, not letting up for even a minute—the farm had been a delight. Small working farms like these managed to thrive by charging an affordable entrance fee, but then having farmhands explain to groups of children how farms worked and how produce ended up on their tables. And of course, there was always the farm shop, where you could buy homegrown organic produce. Even though this particular farm kept the story nice and simple, easy for the kids to understand without going into some of the more brutal details, Marcus could see Katie deep in thought when Charlotte was feeding one of the small pigs or petting a young calf's head.

Fortunately the girls' excitement and enthusiasm made the day for Marcus. Charlotte, in her bright yellow Wellington boots, purposely wading through puddles, reminded Marcus so much of a young Raine. And when Katie gasped on seeing the ponies, Marcus saw immediately how mesmerized she had become.

"Tom, would it be okay for Katie to ride one of the ponies?"

Tom had been keeping an eye on Charlotte, who currently stared mesmerized through the slats of a fence as a woman in dungarees fed a rowdy brood of chickens. When he turned to Marcus, he could not look him in the eyes. "I—uh—I'm not sure," he said, staring past Marcus's shoulder.

At first Marcus thought he understood. When Raine had been alive, she had steadfastly refused the girls riding lessons, citing a young cousin who had fallen and broken his neck in front of her eyes.

"What if I promise to walk alongside her? Keep an eye on her every step of the way?"

"It's not that, Marcus. The ground's slick with rain. What if the pony slips?"

"Ponies are hardy creatures. They're used to all kinds of weather. Tell you what, I'll even pay for the ride."

Eventually Tom caved in. And as promised, Marcus stayed with Katie for the short trip, holding an umbrella over her head. Led by one of the farm staff, they took a very slow walk around the perimeter of the main building. When they came into view again, Tom stood by with Charlotte, the younger sister waving enthusiastically as the pony was led back to the starting point. Tom appeared happy to see Katie's smile of delight.

"There we go. Back in one piece," said Marcus, helping Katie down from the pony. From the look on Charlotte's face, he felt certain she wanted to ask Tom if she could have a ride too. In order to sidetrack her, he immediately called out, "Anybody fancy a cup of hot chocolate and a slice of fruitcake from the farm café?"

"Me," said Charlotte, holding her hand in the air while jumping up and down on the spot.

As they walked toward the small tea shop, the girls together in front holding hands, Marcus turned to Tom and grinned.

"The café treat was a cunning ruse. Because I thought Charlie might ask for her turn on the pony. And that might not have been such a good idea."

Tom continued to move forward, unsmiling, staring ahead at his girls. "She wouldn't have. Katie might like horses, but Charlie's terrified of them."

"Okay," said Marcus with a shrug. "I didn't know that."

"How could you? You're not their father."

For some reason the comment felt coldly dismissive, and Marcus retreated to having minimal interaction with Tom for the rest of their day out.

Naturally, the drive home went by in silence, but happily, this time, without any incidents. When they pulled up outside Tom's house, Marcus fully expected Tom to bid him a cursory farewell after they'd carried both sleeping girls into the house. Marcus settled Katie on an armchair in the living room. From behind him, Tom finally spoke.

"Cup of tea, Marcus?"

"Oh. That would be lovely. Thanks, Tom."

"And I need to talk to you."

"Okay," said Marcus, his heart racing. "Let me just pop upstairs and get the girls a blanket. No doubt they'll be awake before long, but best keep them warm in the meantime."

Heavy footsteps on the stair carpet caught him unaware. He had wanted these few moments to mentally prepare himself for whatever bad news Tom was going to sling at him. Twisting around from his vantage point crouching at the girls' closet door, he witnessed Tom stride into the bedroom and scan the space, bewildered. Below eye level and part hidden behind Katie's bed, Marcus took a moment to study the man. At any other time he would have felt incredibly aroused in the presence of someone whose firm thighs, broad chest, and chiseled chin represented the very essence of masculinity. But he had been at the receiving end of Tom Bradford's foul mood before and wanted no part again. The moment their eyes met and Marcus rose from the floor, the bigger man faltered to a stop.

"Marcus. We need to talk."

When he saw Tom's expression, his heart froze. He knew Tom well enough to know thoughts bubbled beneath the man's surface, but he articulated nothing to allay Marcus's fears. Now he worried that he had messed up again.

"Before you say anything," said Marcus, hoping to preempt the cause of the conversation, his heart pounding, "I want to apologize. I should never have insisted on Katie riding that pony today. Going against Lorraine's wishes. And it was unfair to put you in a position to force the decision."

"I made that choice, not you. And I would do the same again. This is not about that."

In an effort to bolster himself, Marcus folded his arms tightly. Tom's steely expression said everything. This was not going to be an easy conversation, whatever the subject. Marcus felt a dryness in his throat.

"Is this about seeing women?"

"No. Well, yes. Partly."

Maybe Tom could mask his expression, but the flinch of his eyes betrayed the difficulty he was having trying to articulate what he needed to say. Marcus knew he could make things easier if he wanted, but to hell with that. Why should he? Whatever the news, it was clearly not good. Without saying another word, Marcus stood his ground, glaring at Tom, arms folded even tighter, waiting for the other man to speak.

"We're being unfair to you, Marcus. You're doing far too much. Mum thinks we shouldn't be relying on you so heavily. Should give you a chance to find your own life."

"Moira said that?"

"Yes."

"Meaning what, exactly? You don't want me to see you and the girls anymore?"

"No, of course not. Well, perhaps not as much."

"And how do the girls feel about that?"

"They'll be fine."

"And John?"

"What do you mean?"

"What does your father think about his wife's brilliant suggestion?"

"That's beside the point. The fact is I agree with her."

And there it was. One card shown. Tom wanted him to back away. Unable to speak for a few seconds, Marcus was unprepared for how much that declaration hurt.

"This is my life, Tom. Mine to use how I want. Helping you and my goddaughters is my choice, always has been. Even when Raine was alive."

"And you've been amazing. Truly. But having a female presence in their lives, even if it's not their mother, could only be good for the girls."

Another slip. Another card shown.

Marcus could not stop the disappointment showing in his face. Even though he thought he had done well nurturing the girls when Tom could not be there, having the soft touch of a caring woman in their lives someday in the future might be good for them. But not so soon. Maybe Tom sensed Marcus's feelings, because he quickly added, "I haven't seen anyone yet. Call me old-fashioned, but I can only hold feelings for one person at a time. Unlike my teammates at the club, I can't just turn them on and off to suit."

"What is this about, then?"

"I'm doing this for the girls."

"So what?" said Marcus, surprised at the force of emotions that hit him. "My job here's done, is that it? Thanks for playing, Uncle Marcus, but we don't need you around so much anymore?"

"No, that's not what I mean—" said Tom, shaking his head. "Why is this so hard for me?"

"Hard for you?" said Marcus. His eyes burned now, despite attempts to hold his emotions at bay. "If you really want me to back out of your lives, you at least owe me a truthful explanation. Who wants me to back away? Is it your mother?"

"No, Marcus. The decision is wholly mine."

"But why?" he cried before clenching his jaw and stepping into Tom's personal space, causing the bigger man to back away a step. "I love those girls. Like they're my own. And I thought I was helping you. Thought I was making things better, making a difference."

"You are. You have. But—"

"But what?"

"All right," said Tom, gently pushing Marcus away from him. "The problem is mine, okay?"

"With what?"

"With you."

"Me? I don't understand."

"I can't be in the same room as you, Marcus. Not without—"

Marcus felt shame creep across his face and couldn't bear the sudden pause, wanted to fill the silence. What the hell had he done to embarrass the man? Was this about him being gay? Was this about the woman at the water park who thought they were a couple?

"Without what? Come on, Tom," said Marcus, his voice softening to a plea. "Tell me. I thought we were getting along much better now. What did I do?"

"You didn't do—" said Tom, expelling a heavy breath and staring at the ground. Defeated, he leaned against the doorframe, put a hand to his hairline, and pushed a handful of hair back. "For fuck's sake. Why is this so hard?"

"You need to tell me, Tom. Tell me what I did wrong. So I can try to fix it."

"You didn't do anything wrong. And there's nothing to fix. You've just been... *you*. I know it sounds clichéd, but this is really about me, not you. Oh hell, how do I begin?" said Tom, his voice calming as his steady blue eyes met Marcus's. "You're right, we are getting along much better. But the problem is I've—oh shit—I've developed feelings for you, Marcus. Okay? Beyond brotherly affection. And it's confusing the hell out of me. Six weeks ago you left to go traipsing around New York for almost a month. A whole bloody month. Left me trying and failing to do everything for the girls without my copilot. Without my best friend. Felt as though my arm had been amputated. And when you turned up at my mother's house that Sunday you flew back, the moment I chanced to look up and spot you smiling that goofy bloody smile of yours.... Fuck. Something plowed right into me. Thought I'd been run over by an express train. I wanted to leap across the garden, wrap you in my arms, and kiss the life out of you. No matter who was watching. Wanted to throw you over my shoulder, haul you inside, and fuck you senseless. Until you promised never to leave again.

"That night I lay awake, disgusted at myself, wondering what the hell was wrong with me. I told myself that once you were back home for a while and things got back to normal, the feelings would go away. But it's the opposite. Like they've been unleashed into the wild and now I can't haul them back. Lately they're never far from my thoughts. And whenever I see you, they hit me hard. And I'm sick with worry that I might act on them one day and scare you off forever. And I can't let that happen, not again. But if you could just *please* be a little less present in our lives—in *my* life—I might be able to cope better when you're around."

Marcus hadn't realized his mouth was hanging open until his own startled voice sounded. "Fuck, Tom."

Marcus knew he should say something more, but words had abandoned him. Tom, his idea of an ideal man, fancied him? *Him.* Wanted to kiss him? To fuck him? Maybe this could have happened in one of his rare erotic dreams, but in real life?

One look at Tom's tortured expression told Marcus he meant every word. Moreover, Tom would never joke about such a thing. Had Marcus inadvertently given off signals of attraction? If so, he had no idea when, had recently done his damnedest to distance himself from Tom. Besides, Marcus considered himself pretty skilled at letting men know if he was attracted to them. His gaydar rarely let him down. Until this. Worst of all, what was he supposed to do with this little nugget?

"You see. I've disgusted you."

His head lowering, Tom folded his arms around his chest, his misery palpable. Marcus took the opportunity to study this incredibly handsome man he had worshipped for years, while in his head the words "fuck you senseless" kept repeating over and over.

"No, you haven't. I'm just—surprised, maybe, but not disgusted. Shit, Tom, give me a minute to process this—"

"God knows I didn't make it happen. I've only really ever had feelings for one person."

"I know."

"Before Raine, I didn't have any—you know— serious thoughts about anyone else."

"Yes, I know."

"I mean, I dated a couple of women at college, but nothing serious, and I never once contemplated being with a bloke. Not that I think it's wrong or anything, it was just never something I'd—you know—thought about, let alone something I'd want to try. Christ, the male body just isn't aesthetically pleasing like a woman's. Well, apart from yours in those bloody swimmers, which also confused the hell out of me. Shit, this is not coming out right—"

"For fuck's sake, Tom," said Marcus, half laughing. "Shut up a minute, will you?"

"Honestly, Marcus," said Tom, pushing a hand through his hair again and staring at the carpet. "I'm sure that if I ever acted on any of these urges, I'd be as repulsed as you. So can you just let me have the chance to get out there and start seeing women again? See if I can fix this thing inside me? No, I don't want you to stop seeing the girls, but if we could perhaps do less together as a family, see a little less of each other, things might…."

For a fleeting moment, Marcus wondered if he should have taken the opportunity to kiss Tom. But something in his friend's heartfelt plea begged for understanding. And the last thing Marcus wanted to do was scare Tom away completely, to lose his friendship. Because so far, at least, he had been the perfect friend.

"Okay, stop now, Tom. You've made your point. And you should know by now that I'd do anything to see you happy again. So let me talk to Moira. I'll tell her it's my idea, tell her it's to do with workloads. I'm sure we can move the schedule around so we're less dependent on each other. Give you the chance to get out there and mingle in the real world. But please, Tom. One condition."

"Go on."

"Don't treat me any different. I'm still the same friend you can call on whenever you need me. Deal?"

For the first time since he had entered the bedroom, Tom's face brightened. "Deal."

Chapter Ten

OVER the following two months, Marcus almost managed to avoid seeing Tom altogether. Truth be told, Tom laying his emotions on the line had unsettled Marcus. Of course he had always found Tom attractive—a lot of people knew that, even Raine—but as his best friend's husband, the man had always been comfortingly off-limits. Forbidden fruit, so to speak. Yes, he'd had molten private fantasies about the unobtainable husband, but for some reason hearing that Tom had been having carnal thoughts about him had not only thrown him for a loop but frightened the bejesus out of him. What the hell was that all about?

Over time, the distance Tom asked for had worked both ways, and Marcus made a point of sticking tightly to schedules. Occasionally he and Tom would pass each other as one took responsibility for the girls from the other, but then they only had time to share a curt nod or a brief pleasantry. Without Marcus asking or even wanting to know, Moira or the girls kept Marcus updated on Tom's dating progress. In an ideal world, that should have made Marcus feel better, maybe even have given him an incentive to get out there himself. But he didn't live in an ideal world. Far from it. Even so, eventually Marcus turned off the green-eyed monster in his head taunting him with the notion that Tom was out there somewhere with his arm around some random woman.

One consequence of the arrangement was that Marcus had his Sundays back, no more family outings, and could lie in or do whatever he wanted—which was usually nothing. Or worse still, spend time at home stewing over his predicament. At least this week he would have the distraction of a business trip to Birmingham with Tina to sign the lease and get the fit-out started on his new restaurant.

This particular Sunday, however, the special complimentary hotel brunch with Daniel had finally come around. Marcus arrived early and had the pleasure of watching his handsome friend saunter in smiling, turning heads as he descended the three shallow stairs to the reception lectern. He'd chosen to wear a navy suit with an open-necked pale blue shirt. That together with his mop of blond hair made him look more the movie star than ever. After chatting to a clearly smitten waitress, he was led over to Marcus's table.

Barely an hour into the brunch, after they had covered the usual pleasantries and had brought the other up-to-date on their recent career dramas, Daniel put down his fork. Decisively.

"Okay. What's going on with you? If that cloud over your head gets any bigger, I'm getting the waiter to bring over an umbrella."

Although nothing was ever going to happen between them, Daniel had become a firm friend. With him, of all people, Marcus could open up and be himself. For a fleeting moment he thought about telling him the source of his moodiness, but then relented because he felt that wouldn't be fair to Tom. As the thoughts passed through him, Daniel eyed him coolly.

"Let me guess. It has something to do with Tom Bradford?"

Marcus put down his champagne glass and stared at Daniel in disbelief. "How the hell could you possibly know that?"

"Pretty bloody obvious. And I'm guessing that after you tried to restore his trust in his wife's faithfulness with that picture of Stone and his partner, he either didn't believe you or didn't take it so well?"

"I haven't even had the opportunity to tell him yet."

"Why? What has he done?"

Somewhat dramatically, Marcus threw himself back in his seat and let out a big sigh, staring at the huge crystal chandelier above their table, hoping for a *Phantom of the Opera* moment. "He told me he had feelings for me. Ever since I came back from New York. Told me he wanted to take me upstairs and fuck me senseless."

"I see."

Marcus lowered his gaze to meet Daniel's. "You don't sound surprised?"

"You two have been spending a lot of time together. So what did you do?"

"What do you mean, what did I do? I ran a bloody mile, of course."

Daniel laughed before taking a sip of champagne. "Congratulations, Mr. Vine. You've managed a conversion."

"Not funny, Dan. In fact, it's killing me. What am I supposed to do with that?"

"The million-dollar question."

"I've told you what I'm usually like. Everyone's fair game. Dare me enough and I'd take that waiter over there into the toilets right now and blow him," said Marcus, nodding at a young man serving a family of four.

"Heavens, you're making me feel really special today."

"But the thought of doing anything with Tom.... Well. I can't even bring myself to think about it."

"What? You don't fancy him?"

"Of course I bloody fancy him."

"Then I don't see what the problem is."

"That *is* the problem. He's as good as family, Dan. And not only was he horrified about having had those thoughts, he's fundamentally straight."

"Well, clearly that's not the case. Sounds like he might swing both ways."

"And, more to the point, I told him I'd back off. So that he could get out there in the real world and meet some of the fairer sex."

"Very noble of you. And has he?"

"Don't want to think about it."

This time Daniel let out a deep sigh. "I didn't realize quite how fucked-up you are, Vine," he said, getting up from the table to deliver his lecture. "Look, if he's bi, and he's out there trying other women on for size, then chances are he'll either put himself back on the straight and narrow—good expression, that—or if he really can't live without you, you'll have to play the waiting game, give him time to come around. In the meantime, you're just going to have to man up and get on with your life. I'm going to get some more lobster. You need anything?"

"Yeah, a lobotomy, apparently."

"Want a side of Thousand Island with that?"

"Ha-bloody-ha."

While Daniel headed off, Marcus thought about what his friend had said. Yes, he needed to get this stupid notion out of his head and get on with his life. Maybe he could ask Moira and the girls to stop giving him updates on Tom's dating life. Given enough time, he'd be able to cool off and get a grip.

The Blue Royal Hotel had a strict policy about phones being switched to silent during their sumptuous Sunday brunch session, but Marcus had purposely put his on vibrate in case any of his staff needed to contact him. Just as Daniel sat back down, Marcus's phone buzzed. He turned the display over to see the name *Moira* fill the screen.

"You got to be fucking kidding me."

"What is it?"

"Tom's mother."

"Ignore it."

Marcus stared shocked at Daniel as though he had committed treason.

"I can't. I would never forgive myself if something had happened," he said, thumbing the Call button. "Hi, Moira. Is everything okay?"

"Everything's fine. Well, a slight glitch. And a huge favor to ask, I'm afraid. Are you busy this afternoon?"

Marcus peered over the phone at Daniel, who sipped from his champagne flute, assessing the flower arrangement on the table, pretending not to eavesdrop.

"Why? What's happened?" answered Marcus, shrugging and throwing Daniel a world-weary glance.

"I'm babysitting the girls right now. Tom has a second date with this Jeanette woman he met at the cricket club, and they're watching the new Reyna Lockwood film at the cinema this afternoon. She's invited him back to her place afterward for dinner. Apparently she's quite something in the kitchen."

"Is she now?" said Marcus, trying not to sound bitter.

"*You* know what I mean. She's not a maestro chef like you, Marcus, but—"

"No need to explain, Moira. I do understand—"

"The thing is, we need to give her a chance. Give them both a chance. She might be the one who helps Tom build the family back together again—"

"Moira, what did you want?"

"Oh, yes, sorry. Look, John's complaining about a nagging pain in his leg," she said, causing Marcus to smirk at a comment Tom had once made about his father's nagging pain in the arse: Moira. "And I don't want to take any chances, so I'm going to drive him down to A&E at St. Mary's. But you know how long it can take waiting to see someone. And if I bring the girls along, I just know they'll be bored to tears and start climbing the walls within minutes. But I can't leave them here by themselves. Tom would come straight home if I called, but I don't want to spoil his special day. So I wondered if—"

"Give me half an hour."

When Marcus saw Daniel's resigned expression, he almost relented. Instead, he pulled the phone away from his ear and mouthed the words *family emergency*.

"Oh, Marcus, you are a dear" came Moira's voice as Daniel nodded. "If you could pick them up and take them home to their place, I should be back by nine at the very latest."

"Have they had their tea?"

"No, but I can do that when I get there—"

"Don't be daft. If they've been running around your back garden all day, they'll be fast asleep by nine. Don't worry, I'll fix tea for them and make sure they both have baths before bedtime. And I'll get their pack lunches ready for school tomorrow morning. If Katie has her pencil case with her, can you make sure she brings it home? She needs her ruler and pencils for her numbers lesson tomorrow. If you can get them both ready now, I'll pick them up from the front door."

"You are an angel. See you soon."

Even though he was still smiling, Daniel shook his head. "That family owns you. So today's your turn to beat a retreat. One of these days we'll manage to spend a whole meal together."

"You're more than welcome to join me. If you want?"

"Kids, potties, and baths? I'll pass, thanks. Bit too much reality for me," said Daniel, reaching in his pocket for a slip of paper. "And before I forget, you might want to give this number a ring sometime. One of the numbers Ken Villers gave us came up trumps."

BY eight thirty, Marcus had finally managed to get Katie off to sleep when he heard the soft thump of the front door closing. Tom had once complained that his mother had a habit of heading straight for the living room and flicking on the television, which might wake Katie, the lighter sleeper of the two. So after checking on both girls—Charlotte's bedclothes already a mess from her sleep fidgeting—he crept out the door and tiptoed in socked feet down the bedroom stairs. Fortunately, in the small two-up two-down house, carpeted throughout, he could do that quickly and almost silently. But when he reached the second-to-bottom stair and looked toward the door, the figure standing there was not who he had expected.

"Tom?" he said quizzically in a hushed whisper.

Tom stood frozen just inside the door, and even without asking, Marcus could tell something was up. In hugging 501s and the off-white Paul Smith silk shirt Marcus had bought him for Christmas, the top two buttons open, he looked good enough to eat. But the salacious compliment Marcus had been about to let fly froze on his lips. Marcus had lost that right.

"Just managed to get the girls off to sleep," said Marcus, nodding back up the stairs before forcing a quick smile. "I thought Moira was going to come back tonight. Told me you were busy romancing Jeanette."

Marcus had meant to lighten Tom's mood with the words, but they seemed to have the opposite effect. Instead of smiling, Tom scowled and shook his head briefly before looking away.

"Mum texted, but I couldn't call during the film. Phoned and told her I'd come back, even though she tried to insist. She has enough on her plate looking after Dad."

"Is he okay? John? I worry about him sometimes. Especially being pushed around every day by that old woman you call your mother."

"He's fine," said Tom, this time a small smile lightening one side of his mouth as he returned his gaze to Marcus. "Just the bloody arthritis playing up. They're back home now."

Marcus took the brief pause between them to step down into the living room and stand facing Tom. At almost the same moment, Tom tossed his keys onto the hall table and then stepped farther into the room, coming to an abrupt halt.

"Hey. Looking sharp, Mr. Vine," said Tom, his gaze traveling up and down Marcus's body, sending an electric ripple through him. "Were you on a date of your own? Oh shit, tell me we didn't scupper your afternoon?"

Marcus couldn't help the laughter that burst from him. So much for straight men not giving other men compliments. Perhaps Tom had mellowed. Or probably he'd had a few beers over lunch.

"Don't worry about it. More of a boozy brunch with a friend. Catching up on life. How about Jeanette? Was she okay ending the night early?" said Marcus, relaxing a little. "If it'd been me with you dressed to kill like that, I'd have had you handcuffed to the bedposts by now."

As soon as the smart-mouth comment left his lips, Marcus held his breath. But despite a slight darkening of the cheeks, Tom's smile broadened into a chuckle. Yes, the man had definitely chilled. "She was a little disappointed. But she has a six-year-old boy. So she knows the deal of single parenthood."

"And how was it? You know…?"

"Fine. Everything was fine. Not really my kind of thing, but entertaining enough, I suppose. Jeanette seemed to enjoy it, anyway."

Wow, thought Marcus, there's a ringing endorsement. Tom's words came out so flat that Marcus wondered for a second if something had happened. Only then did Marcus realize that Tom was avoiding eye contact again. A silence fell between the two, something both must have noticed, because when they spoke, they did so at the same time.

"Are you okay?" asked Marcus.

"Look, I wanted—" said Tom, before answering Marcus. "I'm fine."

"You don't seem okay."

Another huge sigh shuddered through Tom before he responded. "I'm sick of people scrambling around trying to pair me off. I know they're trying to be kind, trying to help me move on. But I really am fine as I am. Everything's going well and I have everything I need. I really do. It dawned on me while I was sitting there watching that bloody awful film. I have all the women I need in my life, my mother and those little angels sleeping upstairs. And if I want grown-up conversation or advice, I have you and Dad."

"Hold on, Tom. You were the one who asked for time out to go and date. What are you saying now? You've given up?"

"Nobody's ever going to replace Raine, Marcus."

"No, of course not. Nobody is ever meant to. People just want you to be happy again, maybe not in the same way, but at least have someone to share things with."

"And that's what I'm trying to say—" began Tom, but then they heard a soft voice calling "Daddy" from upstairs.

"Shit," said Tom. "I'm sorry. My fault."

"It's fine. You want me to go up?"

"No, let me. Give me a chance to say good night."

Ten minutes later Marcus heard Tom's soft footfalls on the stairs.

"You want a beer?" said Marcus, twisting around and yanking open the fridge door as Tom hit the bottom step. "Got a couple of cold ones in here."

"Actually, another reason I came back is because—" said Tom, hesitating momentarily before going on. "Because I wanted a chat with you."

"Oh, shit," Marcus hissed, two bottles of Asahi in one hand, and quietly closed the fridge door shut, his face falling. "What have I done now?"

Tom appeared genuinely mystified. "Sorry?" he said, taken aback. "What do you mean?"

"Whenever you want to chat with me, it usually means you're either going to tell me to fuck off or back off."

"No, I—" said Tom, his eyebrows scrunched up in confusion, before he deflated with a sigh and gently shook his head. "Is that what you think? Hell, have I really been that much of a dick? After everything you've done for us, for me?"

"You're not a dick, Tom. But you can be bloody stubborn at times. Beer?"

Tom ambled over and took the proffered beer bottle, twisted the lid, and took a long draft. Afterward, visibly relaxing, he perched on the barstool. Marcus went and joined him, leaving a sizable distance between them.

"What I *meant* was, I don't get to hang out with you anymore. And I know that's what I asked for, but in all honesty, I miss it, I miss our little chats."

"Yes, well, whose fault is that?"

"I know, I know. I already claimed the dick card, remember?"

Marcus relaxed too, then leaned forward to clink the neck of his bottle with Tom's. "Well, if it's any consolation, Tom, I miss our grown-up time together too."

And it suddenly dawned on Marcus how much he really had missed just chatting to Tom. If only he could master his infatuation. Maybe now would be a good time to win some points in the friends stakes, tell Tom about Damian Stone, tell him what they had found out. But while the thoughts swirled around in his head, Tom had started talking.

"I really do like that shirt on you, Marcus. Is it cotton?"

"Egyptian cotton," said Marcus absently.

"Looks comfortable. Mind if I...?" Tom held a hand out as if waiting for permission to touch the material.

"Sure. Knock yourself out."

Tom reached across the distance and pinched the material beneath Marcus's collar between his thumb and forefinger.

"This Indian tailor round the back of Edgware Road makes them for me. Has done for a couple of years. If you want, I can—"

When Marcus raised his eyes to meet Tom's, all thoughts left him, the dark heat in that gaze blistering. A sudden memory came back, of Tom sitting on the garden rug, staring angrily at him. Except it had not been anger at all but lust. Instinctively he inhaled a deep breath as Tom fisted the shirt and pulled Marcus out of his chair toward him. Even as Tom brought their mouths together, Marcus hesitated, fully expecting him to recoil, to reevaluate in disgust what he had initiated. But the moment never came. Closemouthed lips pressed onto Marcus's own—firm, urgent, yet still a little unsure. And then, a second later, the essence of Tom Bradford hit Marcus hard, spicy aftershave mixed with Tom's natural body scent and heat, so masculine, intoxicating and addictive. Instinctively Marcus's arms found their way around Tom's neck and he stepped into the man's body, molding himself into the embrace. When he pushed his tongue between Tom's lips, forcing them to part, Marcus took control of the kiss, touching, stroking, exploring, snaking his own tongue around Tom's. In response, Tom shuddered and released a deep moan, before lifting Marcus off the floor and walking him backward until he had him pinned up against the fridge door. Breathless, Marcus pulled his mouth away.

"Well. That's one mystery solved," whispered Tom as he lowered Marcus back to earth, his lips tickling Marcus's ear.

"What do you mean?"

"I wondered if my attraction to you was all in my head" came Tom's husky voice before he thrust his substantial rock-hard groin into Marcus's own arousal. "Apparently not."

Once again Tom sought out Marcus's mouth, more emboldened and self-assured. This time, however, Tom smoothed his palms around Marcus's back, grasping his backside, while he moved his mouth along the line of Marcus's jaw, nipping slowly as he went. Marcus took the opportunity to lift out Tom's shirttails and push his hands up into Tom's chest. Firm, hot stomach muscles gave way to solid pectorals with aroused nipples. When Tom gasped, Marcus almost came where he stood.

"Stay the night," Tom whispered urgently.

"Tom, I can't. We—it wouldn't be right."

"Shit," said Tom, dropping his head on Marcus's shoulder and releasing his hold. "I've misread things, haven't I?"

"What? No!" said Marcus, pulling Tom's head back and kissing him deeply. Once he felt Tom's arms around him again, sensed him relax a little, Marcus brought their gazes together. "Tom, there is nothing in the world I would like more than to spend the night with you. And believe me, if it were only the two of us in the house right now, I'd be ripping your clothes off."

Still confused, Tom followed Marcus's gaze to the rising stairwell. With a soft sigh and a shake of the head, comprehension dawned on him like an avalanche. "You see? This is why I need you around. My common sense guru."

"Wouldn't be fair on the girls. In case they woke during the night."

But the idea had lodged firmly in Tom's head, and he was not letting up. "How about tomorrow? Monday's your day off, and I'm sure I can get a few hours away in the afternoon—"

"I'm in Birmingham until Thursday afternoon, remember? And you've got the girls Thursday night. Friday night you're seeing Brenner and his chums for the UEFA game on the big screen down the Castle. And then Saturday—"

"Fuck Brenner and his chums."

"I'd rather not, if that's all right by you."

But Tom's gaze shone hotly, and he didn't even acknowledge the quip. "Friday night. I'll ask Mum if the girls can stop over. We've got the barbecue in their back garden the next day. Please tell me you're free."

Marcus beamed at the eagerness of Tom's plea. Friday nights remained the busiest night of the week in both restaurants. He'd purposely planned to be back in London on Thursday so that he could be in the kitchen on Friday. But as a precaution, he had also asked both chefs to make arrangements for Friday and Saturday nights in case the deal in Birmingham dragged on. And this was not an opportunity he wanted to pass up.

"I'll make sure I am. But not here, Tom. Come to my place. I'll cook a TV dinner. And after we've watched the game on my hundred-inch flat-screen, I will lead you to my bedroom and teach you some of the ways of the dark side. As long as you promise to stay the night. How does that sound?"

Instead of replying, Tom lowered his grinning lips again onto Marcus's but kissed less urgently this time, his tongue gently exploring Marcus's mouth, his body still crushing rhythmically against Marcus, causing bottles to clink softly in the fridge behind him. Then Tom transferred his attention to Marcus's ears, and his hungry mouth started flicking hotly around his left lobe and then nipping gently at his neck. Just as Marcus had made up his mind that he would give Tom the best blow job of his life, a voice sounded faintly from abovestairs again.

"Daddy."

"You need to let me go now, Tom," said Marcus, twisting out of Tom's reach and heading for the front door.

"Friday," said Tom. "What time?"

"How does seven sound?"

"Perfect. Prepare to have your world rocked, Mr. Vine."

Little could he know, but those words would echo around Marcus's head for the whole of the following week.

Chapter Eleven

ELEVEN thirty Wednesday night, Marcus lay on top of the thick cotton quilt in his hotel room in Birmingham, mulling over the lease signing meeting, which had gone so much better than expected. As usual, a lot of the negotiation points had been complicated, but since the opening of Shepherd's Bush three years ago, he surprised himself at how much he now understood. Nevertheless, that kind of detail bored him—Marcus preferred to be holed up in the kitchen, playing with knives and fire and creating magic.

Which was one of the reasons he had excused himself to use the washroom on Tuesday during a particularly long and arduous debate on renewal clauses. Wandering the corridors of the large law firm, he had tried one door after another until he had stumbled upon a fully kitted-out kitchen. Inside, one of the suits from the firm, taking a break to use the snazzy Italian coffee machine, had explained that the kitchen was only ever really used for firm functions. After getting directions to the toilets from the guy, and then having a quick snoop around the surprisingly well-equipped kitchen, he had found his way to the restroom. And as he had pulled out his phone to check messages, the small piece of paper Daniel had given him fell out of his pocket. On impulse, he'd decided to give the number a ring.

"Brackley Moor Manor House. How may I help you?"

"Yes, hello. May I speak to Laura Kitchener in bookings?"

"Speaking."

"Yes, hello there. My name's Marcus Vine."

After a slight pause at the end of the phone, the woman continued.

"Marcus Vine?" A touch of suspicion crept into the tone. "As in the well-known chef?"

"It is, actually. But I wouldn't exactly call myself famous."

"Oh my goodness, it *is* you. I would recognize your voice anywhere. My husband and I saw you on the celebrity chef feature on Channel Four on Tuesday. We've been to your Edgware Road restaurant three times. Every time the food has been amazing. We're both huge fans."

"I'm honored. And thank you so much for your support. The thing is, Laura—is it okay to call you Laura?"

"Of course! Oh my goodness. Wait until I tell Bobby, my husband, that you called here."

"The thing is, Laura, a good friend of mine made a booking at Brackley Moor around eighteen months ago. I just wondered if you'd have kept any details. Her name is—was—Mrs. Lorraine Bradford."

"Yes, I certainly do. A policeman asked me the same question recently. Told me what had happened to her. And he also said a friend of his might call, but I never imagined it would be you."

"Police Sergeant Mosborough? Yes, we're good friends."

"That's the one. Mrs. Bradford—God rest her soul—placed a tentative booking for the second Saturday of last November. A hundred people. Said it was for a seventieth birthday party. But we never received the deposit or any follow-up confirmation, so we naturally had to let the booking go, I'm afraid. Don't tell me you were going to do the catering?"

"No," Marcus laughed.

When he returned to the boardroom, Tina had been on fire and had already managed to negotiate everything he'd wanted within budget, down to the kitchen overhaul and structural modifications to the shop front. Once the legal paperwork had been signed, they had estimated opening a month earlier than planned. Which was why Marcus surprised them all that lunchtime by slipping out early to cook everyone a hot lunch selection from his new menu, using their underutilized kitchen—he'd bought all the ingredients on his way back to the hotel—a nice change from cold sandwiches, and much to the delight of those gathered.

After the high of the day before came the bombshells from Tina the next morning. Not only had eager American shareholders been in touch overnight wanting to kick off the New York venture, requesting Marcus to be physically there in the kitchen for the first few months of opening, but Millstone Publishing had sent an email requiring his approval of the first draft of his very own Old Country recipe book. With that, came the deadline of getting everything ready for the Christmas market. Typical of Marcus's life, everything seemed to happen at once. Stress he was used to, having worked in a kitchen for most of his adult years, but right now work was becoming overwhelming, and that unsettled him.

Just then his phoned beeped with a message.

U awake?

Tom. And just like that, he found himself smiling and his spirits lifting as his thumbs flashed eagerly across the keys.

Nope. Fast asleep. What's up?

Cant sleep. Keep thinking.

About?

Friday night and what I'm going to do to u.

Marcus gulped, even as his heart sped up. He still had trouble processing Tom's feelings for him.

U still there?

You're killing me Tom.

Killing isnt what I have in mind. Can I call you?

You know you can. Anytime.

Seconds later the phone rang and Tom's deep breathing came down the line. Before he could prepare himself, Marcus's erection began stretching his sweatpants.

"Good evening, Thomas Bradford. To what do I owe the pleasure? You want me to count sheep with you?"

Tom's deep laughter rumbled pleasantly down the phone. "You know something, Marcus? Just hearing your voice does it for me these days."

Marcus smiled and his neck warmed. For all Tom's past insensitive behavior, every now and then he had a way of stalling Marcus with his frank and honest sentiment. "And to think you were going to dump me."

"Shit. We both know I was wrong."

"Tossed out with the garbage."

"Not going to let me forget that, are you?"

"Not on your life."

Tom's chuckle warmed Marcus to the core.

"By the way, Tom, don't forget Katie has to take a cake tin to school tomorrow."

"Shit. Where—?"

"I've put it in the cupboard beneath the sink. In the blue recycled shopping bag. Don't worry, she'll remind you in the morning. And Charlie has her piano lesson after school. But I've arranged for Moira—"

"Marcus—"

"—to pick her—what?"

"I'm losing my erection with all this baby talk."

"You've got a hard-on?"

"Rock solid."

"Fuck," said Marcus before groaning softly into the phone and throwing himself into the pile of pillows along the headboard. "Now I wish I was there."

"You are. Just keep talking. But please, no more cake tins or piano lessons."

"What, then?"

"Whatever. Ask me what I'm wearing?"

Marcus pulled the phone away and stared at the display. Did Tom want to have phone sex with him? Ah well, in for a penny…. "So, what are you wearing, Thomas Bradford?"

"Tonight, sweat bottoms and a T-shirt. In case the girls call for me in the middle of the night. But I'm planning on leaving them at home when I come to you on Friday."

"Christ, I'm so nervous about Friday."

"Why?"

"I'm worried I won't be enough for you. Or that as soon as I see you naked, I'll embarrass myself."

"Now that I would pay to see."

"I'm serious, Tom. I want it to be really special for you."

"It will be. Stop worrying. You're the one with the man-on-man experience. Although I admit, I have been doing some homework."

"Oh yes?"

"Internet."

"I'm listening."

"Went onto a couple of gay porn sites with guys going for it. To be honest, it didn't really do anything for me at first. Not until I stumbled on one guy built a lot like you. Totally different face, but when I covered that with my hand and thought of you... well, let's just say we definitely had liftoff. And now I can think of nothing else. Certainly gave me some ideas for Friday. So come on, talk to me. If I was with you now, what would *you* like to do to *me*?"

And there it was. In reality, Marcus would have liked to have tapped Tom's fine ass on Friday, but he knew the idea might freak the man. In his early twenties, Marcus had bottomed twice, but both times he'd never really felt it, not the way some of his bottom partners had, rolling their eyes back, genuinely aroused and stimulated beneath him. Maybe that's simply how he was built. Or maybe he'd never been with the right man. But if that's what it took to get Tom Bradford in his bed, then he would get himself physically—and, moreover, mentally—prepared. Still, there was something else he had always wanted to do to Tom Bradford.

"I'd pull down your sweat bottoms and suck you dry."

"Details. Give me details."

"Tom. Can we have real sex before we get into the phone variety?"

"Spoilsport."

"Not really. I want to know what sex with you actually feels like before we resort to talking about it. You know, I want to know what it's like with our hot bodies wrapped around each other, or to suck you into my hot moist mouth while my lips squeeze around the head of your cock and my tongue caresses around the salty head before I take you deep in my throat and swallow hard. Or the sensation of straddling your lap with you buried deep inside me. Especially while I'm lubed up and nuzzling your ear and neck, or licking and biting your hardened nipples while I ride you home like a seasoned jockey. Should I go on?"

Tom's ragged voice came down the phone. "You bastard."

"Gay phone sex is a breeze. It's the real deal beneath the sheets that matters."

They both fell silent for a moment, Marcus enjoying the simple sound of Tom breathing down the phone.

"Can I ask you something else?" came Tom's voice.

"Anything."

"Why were you never with anyone? In all the time we knew you, I don't think you ever introduced us to anyone."

"Nobody fancied me."

"Bullshit. I don't believe that for a second. What's the real reason?"

"Honestly? I did meet a couple of people, but none were keepers. Maybe it's because no matter how I tried, I never found anyone who lived up to you and Raine?"

"So what? It was our fault? We ruined you?"

"You didn't ruin me, but—I don't know—everyone needs role models, something to aspire to. And you two did set the bar pretty bloody high."

At the mention of Tom's late wife, Marcus thought back to the telephone call he had made the previous day.

"Tom, how old is your father?"

"Seventy-three. Why?"

"And Moira's sixty-nine, yes?"

"Yes. Why the interest? Is this about their anniversary?"

"What anniversary?"

"They'll have been married fifty years this year. But if you were thinking about offering to do something special for them, they've already said they don't want anything overelaborate. Just a small dinner with close friends and family."

Marcus mulled the words over, wondering if now would be a good time to tell Tom what he'd found out about the day Raine died. Whether wise or not, he decided against it, not wanting to ruin the intimate moment they were having together. As though he'd heard Marcus's thoughts, Tom's voice came down the phone.

"I wish you were here. Lying next to me."

"So do I."

"Are we still good for seven on Friday?"

"Yes. I'm off the whole day."

"As long as you're on the whole night."

"Night, Tom."

Chapter Twelve

JUST before six, an hour earlier than their planned time, a knock came at the door to Marcus's second-floor apartment. In the midst of chewing on a handpicked mint leaf from his windowsill herb garden, he looked up and froze, his stomach churning like a KitchenAid. Absorbed in his food creation mode—he had been assembling slices of marinated apple on top of pastry in a flan dish—he hadn't even showered or spruced himself up. For a moment he wondered if his wooden spoon wall clock—a Christmas present from Katie and Charlie—had run out of battery, but then he noticed the second hand still merrily circling the clockface. Wiping his hands on a nearby tea towel, he decided the caller had to be Ruth, the neighbor from across the hall, probably returning his juicer. She'd said she might pop by at the weekend, and in his book, anyway, Friday was part of the weekend. Besides, Tom couldn't get in without either keying in the entry code or using the video phone at the main entrance. Marcus padded barefoot over to the door and yanked it open.

Decked out in a navy boiler suit mottled with the speckled detritus of past building jobs, and wearing a tight white T-shirt beneath, showing off his bulging biceps, Tom lounged against the doorjamb dressed like every gay man's fantasy. Dark fringed, with trademark slim-line sideburns, he also wore a five-o'clock shadow and was a vision to behold. Of its own volition, Marcus's jaw dropped at the sight, turning him temporarily mute.

"Your downstairs neighbor let me in. Think she thought I was here to fix your plumbing. Or maybe she thought I was there to fix hers," said Tom, chuckling nervously. Sporting a handsome but unsure grin, he looked down at his own attire. "Shit, yeah, sorry. Came straight from work. Been a crazy busy couple of days. Hope you don't mind if I change here, maybe jump in the shower first. Got a change of clothes and a pack of London Pride in the holdall. Although if you'd prefer wine, I can always—"

"Slow down, Tom. And come on in."

Marcus began to head down the hall but turned to find Tom still standing there. "Are you okay?"

Tom had his hand on the door handle, his voice seeming to have deserted him. Marcus noticed the hesitation in his face.

"Oh God, are you having second thoughts?"

"I'm—no—I just…. It's all suddenly become very real."

"Tom, it's me. I'm still your friend. If you just want to have some grub, a couple of beers, and watch the game, I'll be just as happy. And I can always sleep on the couch."

Clearly Marcus would not be happy, but he couldn't stand to watch Tom's discomfort in his own home. Tom seemed to think the words over. "Really? You'd be okay with that?"

"If it gets you in the door, then yes," said Marcus. For some reason a sudden rush of his own nerves rose to the surface. If he was going to be totally honest with himself, after hearing nothing from Tom all that day or the day before, he'd wondered if the man would show up at all. "Come on in and shut the door."

"Thanks," said Tom, entering, then turning quizzically to Marcus. "Are *you* okay?"

"No, it's nothing. You're fine. I—I just…. You're a little early. And you caught me in the middle of prepping," said Marcus, about to head back to the kitchen.

"Hey, hey," said Tom, catching his arm and pulling him back, a playful grin on his face. "I really want to be here. Just give me a little time to adjust. Can you do that?"

"Take all the time you need," said Marcus, and he could not help the overwhelming emotion that overtook him, feeling his own features relax while staring at this man he had admired for so many years. Tom sucked in a sharp breath, dropped his bag, and then turned Marcus around so that Marcus's back pressed up against the hallway wall. Stepping in close, he brought their foreheads together.

"I've had an erection the whole week thinking about tonight," he murmured while grinding their groins together.

Marcus froze for a second before really taking Tom in. Despite the initial anxiousness, tonight there stood before him a confident, masculine sexual beast who, quite frankly, Marcus found both attractive and intimidating.

"I would answer that, but I'm giving you time to adjust."

After a soft chuckle, Tom dropped his gaze to Marcus's lips, and he only hesitated a split second before finding his target. Lips sealed together, Tom pushed his tongue past Marcus's teeth, rushing to meet Marcus's. Of their own volition, Marcus's arms wrapped around Tom's neck, pulling him closer, his head tilting to deepen the kiss. Before long Marcus pushed away, gasping for breath.

"Mmm," murmured Tom, breathing heavily. "You taste of mint and apple. You know, I never thought I'd enjoy kissing another man. But you're all I can think of these days."

"I still can't believe this is you. Tom Bradford. About to get naked in my apartment," said Marcus, stroking a hand over Tom's rough stubble. "Fuck me."

"That is part of the plan," said Tom, smiling, but then stopped when he saw Marcus's expression. "Are you okay?"

"Yeah," said Marcus, but his face had given him away. "Of course."

"As you say, we don't have to actually do the deed, Marcus."

"I know. But I want you to have me. It's just… been a while."

"Then I'll follow your lead. And you can start by taking me to your bathroom so I can grab a shower."

"How about *we* can grab a shower?" said Marcus, pulling Tom with him. "The main bathroom's off my bedroom, so you can dump your stuff there. And then I'm going to undress you."

"How about we undress each other?"

Which is exactly what they did, each of them kissing newly exposed flesh on the other's body, until they stood opposite one another in only underpants. Marcus was the first to reach for the band of Tom's white briefs and gently pull them down. The huge member that bounced out thick and proud took Marcus's breath away.

"Fuck, Tom," said Marcus, his eyes wide. Without a second thought, he fell to his knees, wrapping a fist around the girth and beaming up at Tom. "You've got a lot going on down here."

Tom's laughter was cut short when Marcus pulled back the foreskin and swallowed Tom into his mouth. In the past, Marcus had always taken pride in the fact that he could deep-throat any man. But Tom Bradford would be a challenge. Nevertheless, he took as much as he could, feeling the velvety head nudge the back of his throat. With one hand, he stroked the length while the other caressed and squeezed one ball, then the other and then tugged both. After a number of times, Tom growled, pushing his hips forward and starting to meet him halfway, his hands clamping into Marcus's hair. Although Marcus had thought it impossible, Tom's cock appeared to grow even bigger. But Marcus's mouth had loosened up now, and after releasing Tom with a pop, he took the big guy down almost to the base, sucking hard, even though his jaw ached.

"Shit. Shit. Stop, Marcus" came Tom's raspy voice above him as he yanked Marcus's head away by the hair. "I'm right on the verge. And I don't want to come yet. Stand up."

When Marcus drew level, Tom's eyes had a happy but glazed look. When he pulled Marcus into his body, melded their mouths together again, Tom smoothed his hands down Marcus's shoulders, down his back, under his waistband, and clamped them on each of his cheeks before pulling his underpants down.

This time, finally naked, Marcus led them past the bathtub into the shower cubicle and let the water run. Once it was hot enough, Marcus pushed Tom beneath the flow while instantly Tom pulled Marcus to him, bringing their bodies and mouths together. Marcus's cock finally got to say hello to Tom's. Without prompting, Tom wrapped his hand around both their shafts, Marcus on top, Tom beneath, his hand big enough to grasp them both. Then he began the slow pump, the pull and push, sending a guttural moan of pleasure through Marcus. Still lip-locked, Marcus reached out blindly for the small bottle of liquid shower gel, squirting some on their joined cocks to add lubrication. After that he began to lather Tom's body, never once breaking the kiss. With his soapy hands he explored the hard planes of Tom's body: the rippled stomach, the firm pectorals, beneath his armpits and down his biceps, all the time kissing hungrily. Even when Tom reached around Marcus, smoothed into the valley between his buttocks, causing him to gasp aloud, Marcus continued his own exploration.

Maybe because of the earlier blow job, Tom soon began to pump faster, more erratically, a moan starting deep within his chest. Seconds later his whole body shuddered as he shot warm cum onto Marcus's balls and down his legs. Marcus broke the kiss to watch and almost immediately followed suit, coming onto Tom's stomach and into his pubic hair.

Both men leaned against each other for support, letting the warm water wash over them. Eventually, still unspeaking, they began to clean up. Tom's large hands moving over him felt wonderful and soon had Marcus up and running again. And a quick glance down told him that the exchange was mutual. But Marcus had other ideas.

"Tom, we have all night," he said, switching off the water, stepping out, and turning to face the man. "Let's grab a beer, some food, and relax."

"Did anyone ever tell you your nipples are huge when you're turned on?" said Tom, reaching out and tweaking them, making Marcus flinch and swat Tom's hands away.

"Hands off, tiger," he said, grabbing two plump white towels from the rack and throwing one at Tom. "Beer, food, and Arsenal. Then we can do anything you want. Deal?"

"Deal."

After finishing a dish of homemade cottage pie, organic carrots, freshly shucked peas, and homemade gravy, they sat together on Marcus's leather sofa, watching the game. Both wore only sweatpants and T-shirts; both rested their bare feet on the coffee table. More than once, seeing Tom's big feet next to his, Marcus told himself that he could get used to this. He also smiled at how Tom focused single-mindedly on the television every time action mounted, when one of the forwards managed to breach the opponents' defense, but then, during the many lulls in the game, peripherally at least, Marcus could feel Tom's hot gaze back on him. During short bursts of commercials, Tom never missed an opportunity to lean into Marcus and kiss him, wrapping a hand around his upper thigh, stroking his thumb across his groin. And then, the second the full-time whistle blew, Tom yanked the beer bottle from Marcus's hand and pulled him up from the couch. No hesitation. He dragged Marcus back to the bedroom, where he immediately began pulling Marcus's T-shirt off.

"Whoa, slow down there," said Marcus, laughing and pulling away. "Let me get lube and condoms from the bathroom."

"Condoms?" asked Tom, his brow wrinkling. "What? Are we back in college?"

"Seriously, Tom. Although I get tested after every sexual partner—not that there've been many recently—I don't want to take any chances. And this thing we have between us might not end up being what you want, so we should play safe for now."

"It is what I want," said Tom quietly.

"Let's see how you feel in the morning, shall we? In the meantime, condoms."

When Marcus returned from the bathroom, Tom stood there completely naked and very definitely semierect. One amazing specimen of a man. Marcus placed the lube, box of condoms, and a small towel on the bedside cabinet. This was going to happen, but before passion swallowed them up again, he needed to set some ground rules.

"Another thing," added Marcus, shucking out of his own clothes. "You've got a lot going on down there, so you'll need to let me take control first time around."

"Take control how?"

"Well, we could do this doggy style—nice and slow, though, with me on all fours and you behind—"

"No. I need to see your face."

"Okay, then. Well, in that case you'll need to lie on your back, I'll straddle you, and then you let me take you inside—slowly, at my own pace. Then once I'm comfortable, once I've gotten used to having all of you in me and I've relaxed into a rhythm, I'll let you take over. Are you okay with that?"

The darkened eyes and slow grin that spread across Tom's face said everything, but he kept his voice low. "Yeah. I think I can manage that."

For the next fifteen minutes, they reacquainted themselves with each other's bodies, slower this time, but eventually Marcus decided to take over. After gently guiding Tom onto his back, Marcus helped get the condom on and then prepared himself with an overgenerous coating of lube. Straddling Tom, looking into those dark concerned eyes, he reached down and positioned the head of Tom's cock against his entrance. Eyes closed, Marcus took a deep breath and began to take Tom inside. Just as the initial burn had begun to subside, Tom caressed his arms until he had both hands held in his own.

"Marcus, you don't have to—"

"Hush, Tom," said Marcus, eyes still squeezed closed. "I want this."

After another deep breath, Marcus sank lower until he felt all of Tom's considerable length buried inside him. Sweat beaded his brow and his own erection had taken a vacation, but he had managed to mount all of Tom. And then something happened. Unmoving all this time, Tom's hips suddenly bucked upward and ignited something explosive deep inside Marcus, causing his eyes to fly open.

"Fuck, Tom," he gasped. "What did you just do?"

"Oh, God, I'm sorry—"

"No. Fuck. Do it again."

Tom obeyed instantly, bucked his hips, and once again the lightning bolt of pleasure fizzled through Marcus's body. Not only that, but suddenly his cock had started to awaken.

"Work with me, Tom. As I lift off you and come back down, meet me halfway."

Each time they did this, moving to a mutual rhythm, the pleasure became almost unbearable. Marcus's cock grew painfully erect.

"Swap places, Tom. Can you get me under you?"

Tom, brought out from his own carnal trance, needed no prompting. With ease, and without even pulling out, Tom lifted Marcus and deposited him on his back on the mattress. As Marcus wrapped his legs around Tom's back, Tom moved in for a kiss before starting the solid rhythm again.

"Harder, Tom," cried Marcus. "Give me as much as you've got."

But this time Tom ignored him and took complete control, alternating strokes between short and long, driving Marcus crazy. To get better access, Tom pulled Marcus's ankles onto his shoulders. When Tom finally started to build to orgasm, pounding Marcus long and hard, Marcus lost control and, without even touching himself, shot a huge load between them. Not far behind, Tom growled long and loud, eventually collapsing on top of Marcus.

They stayed that way for a few minutes until Marcus could barely breathe under the weight. Tom must have realized instinctively, because he leaned up on his elbows, slowly and carefully withdrawing his cock from inside Marcus, and then rolled to one side. In the past, partners had mentioned the loss of having someone inside being worse than the initial pain of entry. For the first time in his life, Marcus understood what they had meant.

"Are you okay, Tom?"

When Marcus looked over, Tom was smiling contentedly at the ceiling, like a lion that had just feasted on a kill. "More than," he said. "How about you?"

"Totally confused. I think I must have been doing something wrong all these years," said Marcus, almost a whisper.

Next to him, Tom turned his head to gaze at Marcus. "How so?"

"Let's just say that I've always thought of myself as the top. I'm usually the one doing the fucking. The few times anyone has fucked me, I've never really felt anything."

Tom's face turned thoughtful then. "You didn't enjoy that?"

"Are you kidding me? Were you even watching? You and your magic cock have just turned me into a bottom. I fucking loved what we just did. That was, without doubt, the most intense orgasm I've ever had. Hands-free too. Just one thing, as long as you're up for it."

"What's that?" said Tom, his brow crinkling.

"We'll need to try that at least a couple more times tonight. Just to make sure it wasn't a fluke."

Marcus's heart warmed at the lustful smile that transformed Tom's face. "Count me in."

That night, as they prepared to sleep in the same bed, Marcus marveled at how relaxed Tom had become. Marcus donned his dressing gown and purposely took his time switching off lights in the apartment to allow Tom to pick the side of the bed he was most comfortable with. Marcus didn't have a preference; he often ended up sleeping on the couch after a late night. And when he returned, as he had hoped, Tom sat up in bed on the right side. Marcus smiled, undressed, and climbed in next to him. When they both settled in to sleep, Tom pulled Marcus into him and spooned him into his body, an arm around his waist.

"Night, Marcus," he said, his warm breath on Marcus's neck.

"Back at you," said Marcus.

Just before he dropped off to sleep, feeling cradled, safe, and cared for, a little thought popped into his head.

He could get used to this.

"I'D forgotten you have that huge cast-iron bath."

That morning, Marcus had woken to someone nibbling his earlobe and something hot and hard nudging his backside. When his hand went behind him, he found that Tom had already slipped on a condom and smothered the whole thing in lube. What a way to wake up, and once again Tom managed to wring an earth-shattering orgasm out of him. When Tom had wandered into the bathroom to get a cloth to clean up with, Marcus had followed and now stood behind him.

"It's a claw-foot vintage tub. You want me to run you a bath?"

Marcus enjoyed an occasional soak in the tub, especially after being on his feet all day in the kitchen. With the chrome taps, faucet, and showerhead attachment fitted along the wall side, the tub allowed Marcus to sit at either end of the tub or for two people to sit comfortably facing each other. Not that he had ever had anyone else in there with him.

"Only if you join me."

Until now.

Marcus started the bath running, adding a sprinkling of herbal bath salts, and then left Tom to finish off while he returned to the bedroom to tidy the bed. They had woken after nine, and Tom needed to be at his parents' house by eleven to help them start the barbecue. But with Tom enjoying every last drop of downtime, Marcus was only too pleased to oblige. When he returned, the man in question already lounged in the bath, his dark-haired chest glistening. When Marcus started to undress, he felt Tom's lustful gaze on him, and by the time he yanked off his underwear, he already sported an erection.

"Nice" came Tom's raspy voice. "Now hurry up and get in."

Marcus stepped into the other end and dunked beneath the water, sending bathwater spilling over the side of the tub. Once he had surfaced and cleared the hair from his face, he sat back and marveled at having a grinning Tom facing him.

"Get your arse up here," said Tom after a few moments.

In order to give Marcus more room, Tom lifted his right leg and draped it over the rim of the bath, sloshing bathwater onto the already swimming bathroom floor, while Marcus slid up between his thighs. They kissed again, leisurely now, until Tom turned Marcus around and pulled him into his chest.

"You have no idea what it's been like," said Tom, his face nuzzled into Marcus's neck. "I've wanted you for the past three months. I've lain awake thinking what it might be like lying next to you. And it's been killing me."

"You think I don't know what it feels like?" said Marcus, aghast, twisting around and holding Tom's face in his hands. "I've wanted you for the past ten years. Ten bloody years. Ever since I saw you on that football pitch in the rain."

After another long kiss, Marcus settled back into Tom's chest.

"What do you really want, Marcus?"

"This is more than enough for now."

"No, come on. We all have dreams. What do you *really* want?"

"I dunno. Someone to hang out with. Would be really nice if someday in the future, I could find somebody to say 'I do' to."

Tom fell quiet then. And Marcus understood completely. Too much, too soon. One small step at a time.

"But honestly, Tom," said Marcus, placing his arms over the large ones Tom held around Marcus's stomach, "this will do for now."

Chapter Thirteen

SEEING Tom's marmalade Ford Edge SUV parked out front, Marcus felt a tremble of excited anticipation, which increased as he approached the cream front door of Tom's parents' house. Tom had left him no more than an hour ago, but even so, Marcus felt hungry to see him again, to be in his presence, even though Tom had insisted they be on their best behavior. No touching, no longing stares, no tactile giveaways. Tom's parents would be watching. Marcus had almost laughed at the earnestness in Tom's face. First of all, he would never dream of doing anything that might give them away. More importantly, never in a million years would Tom's parents suspect anything.

He knelt to set his cake dish and Tupperware containers down on the doorstep, took a deep breath, and clunked the knocker since as far as he knew, Tom still hadn't fixed the doorbell. Apart from bringing a selection of mini restaurant goodies, he'd baked his trademark apple and almond tart, one Moira raved about. When he heard footsteps inside coming toward the door, he retrieved the items, ready to hand them over to Moira.

Except Tom answered the door, wearing a navy blue chef's apron over the same white polo shirt Marcus had helped flip the collar into place on earlier—and a lustful smile that had Marcus's lower beast stirring.

"Marcus Vine. And what can I do for you?" said Tom with a wink before raising both eyebrows a couple of times in quick succession, an expression that had Marcus grinning broadly and reddening.

"Where should I begin?" murmured Marcus suggestively.

"And why didn't you use the doorbell?" said Tom, leaning in close to Marcus and prodding the button to the left of the open door to produce a pretty ding-dong that echoed back from the kitchen.

Moira's voice called out asking who was there.

"All fixed. Now you can ring my bell any time you want."

"Stop it, Tom," said Marcus but couldn't help grinning. "It's not your bell, anyway."

When Moira called out again, Tom rolled his eyes and huffed out a sigh. "For goodness' sake. It's Marcus, Mum," he called back over his shoulder before lowering his voice to speak to Marcus. "Fuck. I really want to kiss you right now, but as you can tell, the hawk is circling."

"Best behavior, Thomas Bradford. We both agreed. Best behavior."

"Go say your hellos to the folks and guests. Then come help me with the barbecue."

Marcus went to move past Tom, but the big man stayed in the way so that Marcus had to turn with the cake dish and containers out of the way and squeeze past, brushing his arse against Tom's groin. Behind him, a low growl rumbled through Tom. Marcus was about to turn and chastise him again when Moira popped her head around the kitchen door.

"Tom, there's a lot of smoke. Are you sure you've used the right firelighters? Maybe you should let Marcus take over. Hello, Marcus, dear."

Tom muttered an expletive and a few words Marcus couldn't quite make out before rushing past him and heading out the back door.

"Hi, Moira," replied Marcus, strolling into the kitchen, putting down his wares, and giving her a peck on the cheek she tilted toward him. John and Moira had never been tactile, which Marcus assumed to be a family trait. Tom had sometimes shaken his hand or offered an occasional one-handed slap on the shoulder. Not particularly physical. Until last night changed everything. And once again the mere thought of the night's exertions had Marcus's neck turning red and his heart beating faster.

He needed a beer.

"Honestly, I don't know what's gotten into my son this morning. Anybody would think he'd won the lottery, the way he's behaving."

Marcus smiled and headed toward the kitchen door, but Moira stopped him.

"Where do you think you're going?" asked Moira. As though reading his mind, she opened the fridge door and pulled out a can of Carlsberg.

"To help Tom with the barbecue," he said, taking the beer and snapping off the tab. "Or do you need a hand in here?"

"Somebody I want you to meet first."

Without waiting for a response, Moira led him into their small glass conservatory, which overlooked the back garden. A dozen or so guests already stood around chatting and drinking. Tom's father sat in his wheelchair, his back to the windows, drinking a glass of red and chatting with a neighbor. Marcus was about to stop and say hello, but Moira grabbed his forearm and led him to the far end of the room, where a young man stood alone.

"This is Lincoln Prescott. He's Jimmy Prescott's nephew. From number twenty-seven? Just arrived back from Australia. He's looking into starting up his own catering business over here. Keep him company for me while I finish up in the kitchen."

Even before Lincoln opened his mouth, Marcus got a vibe. Decked out in a milky peach polo shirt and beige chinos, he chose to stand alone by the conservatory window. His arms folded, he rested a bottle of lager in the crook of one arm and had been peering out into the garden. Marcus's intuition grew from the way Lincoln turned and took him in, undressed, and assessed him. And the knowing grin that formed as his eyes returned to Marcus's and lingered, studying him without flinching. Was that also a touch of arrogance? And then, like a bucket of cold water in the face, it dawned on Marcus. Moira had already told Lincoln about him, was probably trying to set them up. The cheek of the woman. So Marcus did the only gentlemanly thing: he smiled broadly and held out a hand in welcome.

"I'm Marcus—"

"Vine," said Lincoln, returning the handshake with an ice-cold hand, the one that had been holding the beer. "Yes, I know. You've been something of an inspiration while I worked down under. I kind of like how you've avoided going the telly celebrity route. Ever thought about opening in Melbourne?"

"Nice idea. But I've got more than enough on my plate at the moment. Excuse the pun."

They continued to chat amiably, mainly about Marcus's success and his new openings in New York and Birmingham. Lincoln—"Link"—appeared to have followed Marcus's career from the early days, reciting almost biographically Marcus's rise to fame. He spoke sparingly but animatedly about himself, about his life in Australia, always bringing the conversation back to Marcus, something Marcus found both flattering and a little obsequious. Marcus positioned himself so that from time to time he could sneak a peek over Link's shoulder, out the window to the amazing man who had shared his bed last night. A couple of times Marcus tried to find an excuse to leave, but on each occasion Link managed to keep him there by asking a few more questions. Eventually Marcus found out why, when Link suggested they go for a drink one night the following week. Flummoxed at first, Marcus accepted provisionally, citing potential work demands. But realizing Moira had instigated the head-to-head, he decided this might placate Link. He could always cry off nearer the time.

A good thirty minutes after his arrival, something tugged at his trouser leg. "Uncle Marc" came the serious voice of Charlotte. She stood before them at waist height, frowning, hands on hips. Her pretense at being stern had Marcus smirking, a look not unlike one her late mother used to pull off to perfection.

"What is it, princess?"

"Daddy says you need to come and take over barbecuing now. Before he remakes the burgers and steaks."

Marcus peered through the conservatory window again and could see Tom gazing anxiously toward the kitchen window. Had he sent Charlotte over because he knew what his mother was up to? And if so, was he maybe a little jealous? The notion gave Marcus a delicious twinge of pleasure.

"Remakes the burgers?" asked Link before taking a swig of beer. His question brought Marcus's attention back.

"Cremates," translated Marcus, which instantly had Link spluttering and coughing with laughter. He had a nice laugh, unaffected, one that lit up his face, and even though Marcus was not in the slightest bit interested, he warmed to Link's easy charm. At any other time he might have been intrigued to know more.

"I'd better go. I did volunteer to help out."

DADDY told me to say that," said Charlotte as she led Marcus out the kitchen door down to where Tom hovered over the barbecue, looking hot and bothered.

"I guessed he might have," said Marcus. "But then, I did offer to help."

"Was that your boyfriend?" she asked, in all innocence.

"No, Charlie," said Marcus, chuckling at her bluntness. "I don't have a boyfriend. That man's a relative of Granny's neighbor. I was just trying to make him feel comfortable."

"Good, because Daddy keeps asking where you are."

"Does he now?"

Tom didn't look so much pleased as relieved when he saw Marcus approaching. Not that he couldn't handle the barbecue well enough, but he looked as though he needed a break.

"Can I go back and play with Gemma and Ewan again?" asked Charlotte.

"Yes, off you go," said Tom to her departing back. "But no running and annoying the other guests. Any of you."

With the two of them alone, they gave each other a furtive grin. Marcus quickly brought Tom up to speed.

"Can't believe your mother's trying to hook me up!" said Marcus, taking the tongs from Tom, nudging him out of the way with his hip, and pressing a couple of burgers to see if they were cooked. Beside him, Tom tugged on a beer but said nothing.

"Although from what he said," continued Marcus, "I think he only wants free advice about setting up a business over here. Wants to take me out for a drink and grill me. In the nonbarbecue sense."

After Marcus chuckled alone and turned a few pork-and-herb sausages, he turned to Tom, who had a sad, pensive expression on his face.

"Are you okay?"

"You know what, Marcus? If you want to see people, I have absolutely no right to ask you—"

"For fuck's sake, Tom. Reel it in, will you? Not only did I have the most amazing time just being with you last night, I also had the best sex of my entire life. So if you think I'm going to risk losing that for Link the Twink, then you must be delusional."

"Yeah?" asked Tom, beaming down at the barbecue.

"Big-time," said Marcus, leaning over and bumping shoulders. "When are you free for another round?"

The speed at which Tom's eyes met his and the molten look that settled in them said everything.

All that afternoon, Tom kept finding ways to get close to Marcus, to squeeze past as Marcus washed dishes, brushing against his arse; to reach for something in a high cupboard, which brought his face close to Marcus's ear; or to walk past and purposely smooth the back of his hand against Marcus's groin.

No matter how much Marcus thrilled at these intimate gestures, eventually he had to find a quiet moment to tell Tom to stop before someone noticed.

ONLY six of them sat around the dying embers of the barbecue as the Saturday afternoon sun bled from the sky. Poor little Charlotte had finally succumbed, her exhaustion finally getting the better of her. Stubborn to the end, though, she demanded to be placed in an old pushchair in the sunshine so that she could still be close to everyone. Katie sat at the picnic table, leaning against Moira, reading her book.

"So what did you make of young Lincoln?" asked Moira, straight-faced.

Marcus felt Tom's foot nudge his own under the table and couldn't resist the smirk that twitched his lips. "Seems like a nice kid. Good sense of humor. And he's clearly been around the block."

"What do you mean by that?"

"He's young, but he knows what he's talking about. He doesn't talk—" Marcus wanted to use the word *bullshit* but thought better of it. "He talks sense."

"And?"

"And what?"

"Oh, come on, Marcus. Is he your type or not?"

"Mum!" said Tom.

"For God's sake, woman," said John at the same time.

"Moira, I'm shocked," said Marcus, holding a hand to his chest in mock horror. "Were you trying to set me up? With a complete stranger? He could be a serial killer, for all you know…."

"Don't be ridiculous. His father's a clergyman."

Around the table, the men burst into loud laughter until Tom noticed Charlotte moving in her chair, and shushed them. John took the reins from there, probably to change the subject.

"Manage to get to any games lately, Marcus?"

"Don't get the time, Mr. B. Spend practically all my waking hours either in the restaurants, with my manager, Tina, or with Tom's brood."

Just then Marcus's phone rang. When he pulled the device out, Tina's name appeared on the display.

"Talk of the devil. Tina. Give me a second."

As he rose from the table, Tom caught his eye and winked. The simple expression had his heart fluttering and brought a smile to his lips. At a safe distance, while Tom's father talked about football, Marcus took the call.

"How're you enjoying your rare day off?" she asked.

"Spiffing. Moira tried to hook me up with a neighbor's nephew."

"No!" said Tina, her laughter followed by a fit of coughing. "Spill."

"Nothing to tell. He's far too young. Barely out of nappies."

"And?"

"And what? Oh, please! You think I'm old enough to be anybody's daddy?"

"No, but I think you're too bloody fussy by half."

"What did you want, Tina?"

"Just had a call from Kurt. Everything's back on track. They want you in New York to train and shadow the new chefs for the Brooklyn restaurant week after

next. The good news is, it's not going to be a long haul.
There for the opening and do a bit of publicity. You'll
be flying solo, though. I need to be here to keep my eye
on the refit schedule in Birmingham."

Marcus calculated the dates and then let out a deep
huffy sigh. Sometimes he just couldn't catch a break.
"Bugger. I knew this would happen."

"What?"

"It's just—the girls are off school that week for half-
term. I was going suggest to Tom that we both take a few
days off work. Drive to the coast or something."

"Is everything okay between you two?"

"You could say that, yes. Oh well, doesn't matter
now, does it?"

"So take them."

"Sorry?"

"To New York. Take them with you, Tom and
the girls. You'll have that bloody huge two-bedroom
apartment again sitting empty during the day. There's
plenty for kids to do over there—musical shows, top
of the Empire State, Statue of Liberty, Central Park.
They'll love it. And you'll have a grown-up to talk to
and do things with in the evenings."

Even as her reasoning sank in, Marcus could feel
the heat rising in his throat at the hope, the possibility
of sharing the apartment with Tom. Although with the
girls there, they'd have to be on their best behavior. No
messing around.

Still.

"And remember, it won't all be work, Marcus.
Apart from the opening night, Kurt only needs you in the
kitchen for one afternoon and evening before and after.
But he also insists he wants you to be hands-off after that
so that his chefs can find their feet on their own. Yes, he

needs you to be contactable in case of any cock-ups, but you won't have to be physically there, just near enough to come and put out fires in case of emergencies. I think it's a great idea to bring them with you."

"I'll need to talk to Tom first. Do you think we'll be able to get them a table for the launch?"

"Consider it done. Now tell me I'm a genius."

"You're a genius. Who's paid loads of money."

"To work her arse off for you."

"And I love you for it. So it's obviously a definite yes to me being there. And I'll text you about the other thing later."

"Excellent. Now go and enjoy the rest of your day off."

Back at the table, Tom caught Marcus's eye and winked as he approached. His father appeared to be holding court, as he liked to, talking football again, something about famous Chelsea wins. Moira, having heard the conversation many times before, had decided to start clearing the table.

"Everything okay, Marcus?" John was the first one to speak as Marcus sat among the small group again.

"Hunky-dory, John. Just been confirmed. New York's very first Old Country has its official opening the week after next."

"Oh, Marcus, that's wonderful news," said Moira.

"Are you going to have to be there?" asked Tom quietly. Marcus knew exactly what he was thinking. Was Marcus going to be deserting his best friend again?

"Of course he has to be there," answered Moira before Marcus could speak a word. "It's the launch, for goodness' sake. They'll want the maestro there."

"How long for?"

"No more than a week," said Marcus. Tom's sullen nod had Marcus smiling. When Tom finally looked up and saw Marcus's reaction, he sighed and smiled back.

"Well done. Good for you."

"Thing is, it's over half-term, Tom. Tina's not going to be there, and to be honest, I could use some moral support. I don't suppose you could get some time off work? So you and the girls could come too? I mean I'd have to spend a couple of days and evenings at the restaurant, and you'd have to come and support me by dining there as my guests on the evening of the launch. But they mainly want me on call after that, so I'd be free to join you for outings and fun. And besides, there's plenty for you and the girls to do. Katie always wanted to ride the Staten Island Ferry."

As Marcus spoke, Tom sat up straighter and straighter in his chair, the transformation on his face priceless.

"Oh, I think that's a wonderful idea," said Moira. "But what about flights?"

"We'll transfer Tina's ticket into Tom's name. For the girls, I have so many points I'm never going to spend, might as well put them to good use. And the sponsors always put me up in this huge two-bedroom apartment. So accommodation would be taken care of."

"Two bedrooms?" asked Moira. "How would that work?"

"One for the girls. One for Tom," said Marcus. "And there's this humungous couch in the living room that I'll sleep on."

"That I'll sleep on," said Tom.

"Yes, well," said Marcus, looking directly at Tom but keeping a straight face, "I might have to toss you for that. At the end of the day, Moira, it's more a case of whether Tom wants to come or not."

"Of course he wants to come, don't you, Tom?"

At that moment Tom smiled slyly and sat back in his chair. "I'll have to think about it," he said, making Moira huff in annoyance and Marcus laugh aloud.

"Book the bloody tickets, Marcus," piped in John. "No son of mine is going to look a gift horse in the mouth. And don't your restaurants have English memorabilia on the walls?"

"They do. Not quite Hard Rock Café classics, but some nice British mementos."

"We still have that shirt signed by Ed de Goey, the Chelsea goalkeeper back then, after their FA Cup win back in 2000. The one you won at auction. That would be a fair trade, son."

"You kept that?" asked Tom.

"Course we did. It's not ours to toss. And it's probably worth a few bob."

"You're absolutely right, John," chipped in Marcus. "These things fetch a fortune on eBay. What sort of condition is it in?"

"Take Marcus up to your room and show him, Tom," said John.

"No, it's fine—"

But Tom was already pushing his chair back from the table.

"Come on, Marcus," said Tom, smiling and heading toward the house. "Think you might be really impressed."

"I tucked it behind the headboard. Ignore the mess and the boxes on the bed," called Moira, as house-proud as ever.

Marcus stepped into Tom's old bedroom first while Tom flicked the light on. Marcus stood there, taking in the setting, a little dusty and neglected now, but with a faint smell of adolescent male. He only stood there for a second, though, before being spun around, pinned to the bedroom door, and kissed. When eventually he came up for air, Tom was beaming at him.

"New York. Could this weekend get any better?"

"With the girls, Tom. We'll need to be good."

"We'll make it work. In the meantime, next Wednesday lunchtime."

"What about it?"

"I have a meeting in the morning. Finishes around eleven. I could be at your place by midday as long as I'm back on-site by two thirty. What about it?"

So that was how it was going to be, thought Marcus. Stolen moments. Not that he could complain. He had, after all, told Tom that what they had together was good enough for now. The problem is, nobody ever explains how long "for now" means.

"Done. Anything special you want for lunch?"

"Just you, naked and ready to go when I get there."

Tom leaned in for another kiss, a hand straying down to Marcus's groin.

"I think I can manage that," said Marcus, pushing gently away from Tom. "Now show me this football jersey your father mentioned. Before we both get caught."

Chapter Fourteen

THE week leading up to the New York opening had been hectic. Marcus also had to sign off on plans for the Birmingham refit back in England, ensure the restaurant roster in London was sorted for his time away, and get the results of his medical—something the US investors had insisted upon—which fortunately came back all clear. Apart from work, he and Tom had managed to get together three steamy times; twice in Marcus's apartment over lunch, and another whole night together on Tom's "Friday night with the boys" pub night. And even though Marcus enjoyed their time together—especially the overnights— he was looking forward to doing regular things with Tom and the girls, to being with them together in New York.

Everything had been settled by the time they needed to leave. Tom had managed to get time off work but would need to attend one or two meetings via a web video chat program. Marcus would, of course, be called upon to talk to the press and make appearances in the restaurant whenever requested. But apart from that, they were set to go. Tina's travel agent had arranged four economy seats together on their transatlantic flight flying out that Saturday morning. Although Marcus had to sacrifice his usual business-class luxuries, the payoff was well worth it. Tom and Marcus sat on each of the aisle seats with the girls in between. Both girls behaved perfectly, mesmerized by the airline's entertainment system and cartoon films. Then, as arranged, a car picked them up from JFK and whisked them off to the luxury apartment for the beginning of their seven-night stay.

Everything went perfectly—until they reached the apartment.

"I am not sharing a bed with Charlie, Daddy. I want my own bed. You know what happened last time we went on holiday. She kicked me three times in her sleep and then pulled the covers off the bed."

"Did not."

"Did too."

"Did *not*!"

"How would you know, anyway, stupid? You were asleep."

"Stop it, the pair of you!"

Tom rubbed at the bridge of his nose and breathed deeply. He had made the suggestion to Marcus at Gatwick airport that the two of them share the bedroom with the single beds and the girls could take the super king-size in the other. That way, once the girls were fast asleep, Tom might be able to sneak over during the night for a chat—or whatever.

Until Little Miss Cockblock had decided to scupper their plans.

"This bed is huge, Katie. Charlie's going to be way over the other side."

They all stood in the doorway to the master bedroom, cases still unpacked until the decision was made.

"I don't care. She won't stay there. You know what Granny calls her. Miss Fidget-pot Kickboxer."

"Katie—" began Tom.

"Tom, it's fine. Let the girls have the single beds. I'll sleep on the couch."

"Don't be ridiculous. Neither of us could fit on that thing. Your legs will be dangling over the end, and if I took it, my feet would be touching the floor."

Tom had a point. Funnily enough, Marcus remembered the couch being bigger. But then he'd never had to sleep on the thing. Charlotte didn't help matters by bursting into giggles at the image of Tom or Marcus's feet hanging over the end.

"How about you sleep in here with me, then?" Tom asked Katie.

"I want my *own* bed," said Katie, hands on her hips. "This is so stupid. Why can't you and Uncle Marcus share the big bed? It's made for grown-ups, not for us kids."

For a moment Marcus couldn't believe his ears. He looked eagerly over the girls' heads to Tom, just as Tom spun his gaze around with as much keenness.

"No, *I* want to sleep with Daddy in the big bed," said Charlotte out of the blue. "Can I, Daddy? Can I?"

Tom sighed and smiled down at his daughter before catching Marcus's gaze and giving him an apologetic shrug that said "we're not going to win this one."

"Of course you can, princess. Okay, now that's settled, let's all get unpacked."

Later that evening, with both girls asleep in their separate bedrooms, Tom and Marcus shared some adult time on the couch. But a kiss and cuddle was about all they were going to be allowed.

"I'm really sorry about this, Marcus," said Tom, smoothing his thumb along Marcus's bottom lip, a little habit of Tom's that Marcus had warmed to.

"Not your fault. It's their holiday too. Don't let it spoil things."

"Still," said Tom.

ON Tuesday and Wednesday, the day before and the day of the launch, Marcus had to spend the whole day in the restaurant. Twice Marcus had opened restaurants, so he knew that things rarely went to plan and he needed to be ready to face challenges. Last-minute alterations had to be made to some of the furniture—if there was one thing Marcus couldn't stand, it was tables that wobbled even slightly whenever anything was placed on them— tablecloths and napkins had not been delivered, pictures had yet to be hung on walls. In the kitchen, however, everything seemed to be going well. Kurt had recruited expertly, and the people around Marcus already felt like family, working with and around one another seamlessly, like a well-oiled machine.

By six o'clock on opening day, with all staff— kitchen and front of house—assembled out front, not only had Marcus cooked a range of the menu dishes and specials for all the staff to sample so that they could advise customers on choices with complete and expert authority, but he also gave his customary rousing speech.

At seven o'clock, with everyone at their stations, the doors opened and a steady stream of people entered. In his London restaurants, although most of the tables would be available for booking, he always made sure the remainder were left free for walk-ins. No such luck in New York. Demand had been off the scale, and Kurt had been keen to get bums on seats. Which, of course, meant that the kitchen was soon buzzing with activity. At around nine thirty, Kurt came into the kitchen to find him.

"Marcus," he said, "come on, buddy. Your presence is required. It's showtime."

When Marcus stepped out from the kitchen in his kitchen whites, he was not only met with camera flashes and huge applause, but a couple of people actually rose from their seats to give him a standing ovation. Now *that* had *never* happened in either of his other openings—perhaps this was an American cousin thing—and he instantly felt himself blushing.

After he had spoken to and thanked the many guests and had any number of photos taken with them, he finally made his way over to the table where Tom and the girls sat. Kurt had reserved them one of the booths, which they shared with another couple and their son, a boy around the same age as Katie.

"Uncle Marcus. Are you famous now?" said Charlotte as he approached.

"Is he really your uncle?" asked the boy, aghast, staring at Katie. "Really?"

"Yes, and he cooks for us at home sometimes," said Charlotte proudly. "He went to school with our mummy, but she died. And he's our godfather."

"That is way cool," said the boy.

Marcus came up and gave Charlotte a kiss on the cheek and then Katie. Once finished, he nodded to Tom and shook hands with the two other adults.

"Larry and Karen Flynn," said the man, enthusiastically pumping Marcus's hand. "And this is our son, Bradley. It's an honor to meet you, sir. That was one darned fine meal. My grandmother came from Ireland, and she made a fish pie just like the one you served up today."

"Thank you for those kind words. And that looks suspiciously like my signature carrot cake, Mr. Bradford."

"You know I can't resist," said Tom with a wink. "Larry and Karen are up from Jacksonville. Karen's brother's in *The Lion King* on Broadway. They've been giving us some tips on where to visit while we're here. We've arranged to go up the Empire State together tomorrow. Are you still going to be working?"

Marcus looked around the restaurant and let out a sigh. "Looks like it. Sorry, Tom. We're open for lunch as well tomorrow, so I need to show my face, at least."

ON their last full day, Friday, Marcus finally managed to get some time off, but had agreed to remain in the apartment in case he was required on short notice. Tom and the girls had gone out with the Flynns again, this time to finally ride the Staten Island Ferry. But Tom had warned Marcus that he needed to get back at midday to take an online video call with his client and partner back in the UK early in the afternoon. Marcus could see that they had really warmed to the Flynns and was not surprised when they all came back to the apartment, looking wet and bedraggled.

"Hello, you guys," said Marcus, coming around the bar of the small kitchen. "How was it? I think some of you could use a hot drink, yes?"

A general murmur of assent came from the adults in the group.

"Started off great," said Tom, grimacing. "Until the heavens opened."

"It was brilliant," said Katie, kicking off her boots. "We got lots of photos."

While the clan went about getting out of wet coats, Marcus prepared pots of hot tea with honey and lemon for the kids, mugs of his Kenyan brew coffee for himself and the Flynns, and a mug of strong black tea for Tom.

As they sat around warming their hands on the coffee mugs, each took turns telling him about their morning adventure. Katie especially had fulfilled one of her dreams and also seemed to have made a good friend of young Brad. After a whispered conversation with her husband, Karen, who had noticed Tom glance at his watch a couple of times, chipped into the conversation.

"Tom, the offer's still on. My brother's confirmed as many free tickets as we want to see him in the matinee today. It starts in about an hour's time. Perfect antidote for this weather. I know you said you had to do your work thing, but I wondered if you'd thought any more about letting us take the girls to see the show?"

Tom faltered for a minute, but both Katie and Charlotte pounced on the idea.

"Yes, Daddy," said Katie eagerly, her hands on his knees. "Please say yes."

"We'll have them back by five," said Karen. "And I might even be able to get them backstage to meet my brother and the rest of the cast."

"*Pleeeaaaasssseee*, Daddy," said Charlotte, pulling on his trouser leg.

"If you're absolutely sure," said Tom. "I'd join you too, but I've got this call with the UK—"

"I know," said Larry sympathetically. "But it's their last day and all. And not only would they keep our Brad company, but I'm sure the last thing you need is having bored kids under your feet while you're trying to do business."

"Good point," said Tom before turning to Marcus, a hint of a smile on his face. "And of course they can go."

All of the kids began jumping up and down, yelping for joy. Even though the noise was deafening, Marcus's look of surprise had Tom grinning broadly. Had he planned the whole thing so that they could be alone?

"But don't you want to join them, Marcus?" asked Tom, milking the situation. "I mean, you've barely had any fun time at all."

"No can do, mate," said Marcus, returning a mock grimace. "I'm on call. Could be needed at a moment's notice. So I'm afraid you're going to be stuck with me for the afternoon."

"That's settled, then," said Karen, rising from her seat. "We'll all fit in one cab—if we can get one in this weather—and be in there in fifteen minutes. I'll text my brother and tell him we're on our way."

As soon as the door closed on them, Marcus threw his arms around Tom's neck and pecked him on the lips. "You crafty so-and-so. You orchestrated that, didn't you?"

"Maybe," said Tom, nuzzling Marcus's neck. "Seemed only fair that we finally get some time to ourselves. Agreed?"

"I *so* agree."

"Good. So let me get this conference call out of the way and then I'm all yours. Just give me a couple of minutes," said Tom, releasing Marcus and disappearing into the main bedroom.

Marcus could not believe their luck. Whistling to himself, he kept busy by collecting the cups and mugs around the room and filling the sink with soapy water. While washing up, he sent up a silent prayer that Kurt would not call, that he and Tom could have some private time. When the bedroom door opened, Marcus continued cleaning.

"Marcus" came Tom's deep voice.

When Marcus glanced around, Tom Bradford leaned against the doorjamb, naked except for a pair of brand-new white Calvin Klein briefs—an extremely well-loaded pair of briefs. Marcus dropped the mug he had been rinsing, his mouth falling open. Tom looked incredible, better than any model Marcus had ever seen—would have even given Fereddique a run for his money.

"Come on, baby. We're on the clock," said Tom, beckoning with his forefinger and backing into the bedroom.

"What about your conference call?" said Marcus, unbuttoning his jeans as he headed toward the bedroom.

"Canceled," said Tom, pushing Marcus onto the bed and pulling the jeans off him. "We managed to cover everything yesterday. We've won another contract, so I'm celebrating too. Gonna be a shedload of work for the next six months, but at least we get to keep all our guys busy. Now get the hell naked, will you?"

As Marcus pulled the sweatshirt over his head, he noticed that Tom had already placed condoms and lube on the nightstand. Not that long since their first sexual encounter and Marcus already had Tom well trained. Tom had been about to pull down his own underpants, but Marcus swatted his hands away.

"My job," said Marcus, slowly rolling them down Tom's large hairy thighs, until Tom's cock bounced out, fully engorged and ready for action.

Sitting on the side of the bed with Tom standing in front of him, Marcus took Tom in his mouth, wrapping a hand around the girth. In the short time they had been together, Marcus had learned a lot about Tom, what he enjoyed in bed and what really got his motor running. Above him, Tom's breathing became raspy and—yes— when Marcus moved his hand up to Tom's chest, his nipple was already as stiff as a metal bolt. After sucking both balls into his mouth and pumping the girth a couple of times, Marcus knew Tom would soon take the lead.

Today Marcus sensed an urgency in Tom, a hunger for gratification. Because of their short bursts of time together, this had become something mutual, but even so, Tom was not a selfish lover; he always made sure that Marcus came with him all the way. But today Marcus shared Tom's need. Until Tom did something completely unexpected. Taking Marcus under the arms and lifting him back onto the bed, he climbed on top and straddled Marcus.

"Tom, what are you doing?" said Marcus.

"I want this. I've been thinking about this for a while now. Sometimes I lie awake at night, use some lube, and put my fingers in there, wondering just how you'd feel inside me. Why? Don't you want to?"

"Fuck, yes. Of course I want to. I just need to know you're comfortable doing it."

"Only one way to find out."

Tom went quiet then, and Marcus glanced up into his lustful gaze. Before the man changed his mind, Marcus grabbed a condom, ripped open the foil, and rolled the latex onto himself. Above him, Tom prepared himself with generous amounts of lube. This was going to happen, Marcus told himself.

"Come on, then," said Marcus. "You're in charge. Take your time."

Tom lowered himself onto Marcus, far quicker and surer than Marcus would have believed. Sweat glistened on his brow, but eventually he felt himself fully inside Tom, with Tom's still-erect cock resting on his stomach. With that, Tom leaned forward, placed his large hands on either side of Marcus's head, and kissed him leisurely.

"Tom," said Marcus after a few moments, "you need to start moving."

Tom complied immediately, after a while bouncing up and down on Marcus, each time his huge member slapping Marcus on the stomach. Eventually Marcus could hold on no longer and cried out Tom's name as he shot into the condom.

When they lay next to each other, both panting, Marcus swung his head to examine Tom.

"And?" he asked.

"Interesting," said Tom, who had not climaxed. "Might take a bit of getting used to. Maybe preparing myself better beforehand."

"Let's save that for an overnighter. I can help out there."

"Yes?" said Tom, his eyes lighting.

"Fuck yeah," said Marcus, chuckling. "I would be honored."

"In the meantime," said Tom, reaching out for a condom, "any chance of a fuck?"

Since that first time, Marcus had eagerly looked forward to being fucked by Tom. Something had happened that he'd never experienced before, like trying a type of cuisine you'd never considered before but which now gave you an insatiable appetite. Marcus also let Tom lube him up, loved watching Tom's eagerness.

Before long they rocked into their comfortable rhythm until Tom's pumping motion sped up, becoming more erratic. In Marcus, the electricity built, growing stronger until release overcame him. Orgasms with Tom inside him were so incredibly intense. Next time he had the chance to fuck Tom, he needed make the experience better.

For the next half hour, they lay holding each other, spent. Strange, too, because Marcus had never been a cuddler. Usually after sex, he'd be the first one out of the door. In small ways, Tom was changing him. Intimacy was becoming his friend.

The one to notice the late time, Tom roused them both. Marcus sighed at the inequality of their short time together. But this session had been a first, Tom giving himself to Marcus. Marcus needed to reciprocate, to give something in return.

Tom sat on the edge of the bed, pulling on his trousers. For some reason Marcus felt an overwhelming apprehension, but he knew he had to finally tell Tom what he knew about Damian Stone.

"Tom," said Marcus.

Marcus had only uttered that one word, but Tom must have sensed Marcus's seriousness, because he stopped what he was doing and turned his way.

"Do you remember that policeman friend of mine? From the water park."

Tom said nothing, but his gaze became dark. Whatever he was thinking was probably way off the mark, but Marcus had to keep going now.

"Well, I asked him to do me a favor and try to find out about Damian Stone."

"And?"

"And we found out where he lived. I went there with him to see if we could find anything out. Turns out Damian Stone did go to the same yoga class as Raine. He was also in a committed relationship with another man."

That remark managed to get Tom's full attention. "He was gay?"

"Yup. We spoke to his partner. Damian Stone also moonlighted, a bit of catering on the side. The reason why Raine was in his car that day—at least this is what I assume from everything else I know—is that they were heading down to Chipping Norton to check out a venue for a party."

Tom was staring at the wall now. "Whose party?"

"That's the thing. I still have no idea. The woman at the venue said Raine was arranging a seventieth birthday party, but I don't know anyone—"

Tom had dropped his head into his hands, and Marcus could see his shoulders shaking and hear a soft sobbing. Marcus got up immediately and went to him, put his arm around his shoulders. "Tom?"

"All this time" came Tom's muffled voice.

"I know. But you didn't have all the information."

"How long have you known?"

"Not long. A couple of months. But I didn't have all the facts. I've still no idea who the party was for. Not John or Moira, that's clear."

"You seriously don't know?"

Marcus shook his head and then looked curiously at Tom. "No. Do you?"

"Pretty bloody obvious. The answer's here in this room. The year she died, you were about to turn thirty and—"

"You were turning forty. Shit. You mean the surprise party was for the two of us?"

"And all this time I've had a nagging doubt that maybe, just maybe, she'd betrayed me. When right now, it feels like it's the other way around."

"Don't say that, Tom."

"I asked you to leave this alone, Marcus. I told you I didn't want to know."

"I know. And I'm sorry."

They spent their final evening in New York together at an Italian restaurant with the Flynns and then, after promising to keep in touch, headed back to the apartment. Although Tom remained friendly and civil around the Flynns, he became quiet in Marcus's company.

Even on the flight home the next morning, Tom remained sad and sullen. Despite the success of the New York opening, Tom's reaction to Marcus's admission had tarnished Marcus's jubilation. Should he have kept quiet? Not said anything? But the answer to that was clear. He had a duty to his late best friend and to Tom to set the record straight, even if that meant losing everything he had only recently gained.

Chapter Fifteen

AFTER his admission about Damian Stone, Marcus had thought Tom would disappear into his shell the way he usually did—stop seeing Marcus altogether. What actually happened couldn't have been more different.

During the following month, Tom sought desperately to find time slots for them to be together for sex—and the session heat ramped up to molten levels. But something in Tom had changed. He brought a fierceness to their brief encounters, and sometimes the detached passion unsettled Marcus. Not at the time, because Tom still made every effort to make sure he brought Marcus with him all the way. Neither did he offer to bottom again—not that Marcus minded that. Later, however, in quiet moments, Marcus realized they barely spoke during their lovemaking sessions.

And whenever Marcus did, usually asking if everything was okay as they both quickly dressed to be elsewhere, Tom would placate him with a curt "Stop worrying. Everything's fine."

But other things—barely noticeable at first—had begun to happen. Even though they were having more short-notice encounters, there were no overnight sessions. Tom cited his need to keep his parents from suspecting anything. He'd also canceled once or twice at the last minute due to sudden work engagements—always something that did not form part of the careful household schedule they all followed meticulously. In Tom's defense, his company had been inundated with work—Moira kept Marcus regularly apprised—and they were struggling to meet the deadline on one of the jobs.

Life had a habit of becoming busy when you least expected. Marcus knew that only too well. And while Marcus's restaurants on either side of the Atlantic had reached a nice, manageable stride, giving Marcus more time to get involved in other things—approving the final draft of the recipe book Tina had asked him to create with the ghostwriter, final arrangements for the Birmingham opening—Tom's business had taken on a little too much.

One Thursday, Marcus picked the girls up from school and dropped them off at Moira's because Tom had a work meeting to attend, and she was busy preparing tea for them all. Moira insisted Marcus stay for a cup of tea and a chat. She always had a subtext for any invitation of this nature, and around seven, just as Tom joined them, the truth surfaced.

"Now Marcus, dear. We're having a private dinner to celebrate our fiftieth wedding anniversary. Nothing fancy, about twenty of us—close friends and relatives.

I know you'd probably want us to come to one of your restaurants, but we don't want all the palaver of arranging transport to come uptown. So we're going to Fettuccini on the high street. It's one of John's local favorites. They have a private dining room with easy wheelchair access. So I wondered if you'd like to come and if you'd want to bring anyone. Maybe Lincoln, if he's available?"

Marcus glanced at Tom then, whose gaze dropped uncomfortably to the floor. Moira noticed the exchange.

"You can come alone, if you wish. Tom's bringing someone."

"I see," said Marcus, folding his arms, a sudden anxious feeling in his gut. But he vowed not to show his feelings in front of Tom. "Thank you for the invite, Mrs. B. Yes, I'd be delighted to come. But it'll just be me."

ONE of the downsides of being a celebrated chef was that you also innately became a harsh critic of other people's food. Good value was about the best he could come up with after sampling some of the soggy lasagna, overcooked pasta, and bland, uninspiring sauces on the sharing platters at Fettuccini. When the chef came out to say hello—someone had probably let on that Marcus Vine was in the house—Marcus made pleasant comments about the fare to the jolly Welshman who ran the kitchen.

But John and Moira appeared to enjoy the simple food, and after all, this was their special day. As an anniversary gift, Marcus had bought them tickets to see a show in the local theater, one that Moira had mentioned a couple of times to Katie. All in all, the evening went well, apart from the fact that Tom brought along Jeanette, the woman he had dated before choosing Marcus. Marcus liked her because she spoke her mind and came across as capable. What rattled him was that Tom hadn't mentioned anything to him.

Toward the end of the evening, once most of the guests departed, the five remaining shuffled down to one end of the long table, where John held court in his wheelchair. On the opposite side of the table from Marcus sat Jeanette, with Tom to her left, while Moira sat next to Marcus.

Every now and again, Marcus caught Tom's eye, the two of them sharing a moment of levity at a remark made by one of the guests. With a few drinks inside him, Tom seemed more like his old self. When Tom excused himself to use the bathroom, Marcus allowed conversations to bubble around him while he sat back and checked his phone. A message from Tina caught his eye, to call him about a few nonurgent matters they needed to get sorted. She had also sent him the article by Kitter that would be appearing in the *Observer* tomorrow, which he flicked through quickly. Beautifully written, of course, but more importantly, essentially positive. Knowing he was out that night, Tina had purposely not called. Not difficult to guess what the message was about: a few more interviews, a few more signings, maybe an update on Birmingham. After popping the phone away, he decided to call her the minute he got home. Get business out of the way in case Tom's promise of getting away for an hour or two to pay him a late-night visit materialized.

"Tom seems much happier these days. Did you have anything to do with that?" said John, peering down the table. Having taken a mouthful of water, Marcus lowered the glass from his mouth and was about to reply when Jeanette beat him to the punchline.

"You know, I'd like to think so," she said, tilting her head as she dabbed the corner of her mouth with a napkin. Marcus almost choked on his water. "We had a bit of a rocky start. Both needed time to breathe, I suppose. But yes, I've been out with him a couple of times recently."

"Have you?" said Marcus, unable to stop the words tumbling out. Why had Katie or Charlotte not mentioned that? Or did they even know? More importantly, why hadn't Tom?

"Just tagging along, really. Drinks down the pub with his football friends. And dinner with his work colleagues and their other halves when Tom needed someone on his arm."

Marcus stayed his tongue this time. But unwelcome thoughts began to seep into his head. Was she really only acting as a companion to his formal events? Or was there more?

"Been trying to persuade him to take a weekend break with his girls and my son, James. They're around the same age. If only I could get him to take some time off. He works so hard. Almost missed Katie's parent-teacher evening."

Perfect timing: the man in question returned to his seat at that moment.

"You took Jeanette to Katie's open evening?" asked Moira, surprised, preempting Marcus, who had been about to ask the same thing. "You never said anything."

Taking his seat, Tom simply shrugged but offered no explanation.

"Oh, I didn't mind," said Jeanette after a quick glance at Tom, clearly sensing she had stumbled upon something contentious. "James is in the year below Katie, so we did each other a favor, really. Anyway, the teacher we saw— Miss Stewart—seemed to be really impressed with Katie."

"I thought Colbert was Katie's homeroom teacher?" asked Marcus, glaring at Tom. "Doesn't Stewart only take her for numbers? Why didn't you—"

"Colbert was sick," interrupted Tom, returning Marcus's fierce gaze.

"Then why not reschedule?" asked Marcus softly, but Jeanette had already continued on, the poor woman floundering in the wake of Tom's reticence.

"She had nothing but good things to say. A super bright girl, she called her. Said she'd always been good at reading and writing but had struggled with basic arithmetic. And then mentioned how much she had improved over the past term."

Yes, thought Marcus, thanks to my hours of tutoring and perseverance. Even a cursory glance told him that Tom could read his bubbling anger.

"And now you're considering a weekend break with Jeanette and James, I hear?" Marcus said, directly to Tom.

"Nothing's decided yet," said Tom, glaring back at Marcus. "Depends on a whole lot of things. Work, timing, school holidays."

"Sounds lovely," said Moira.

Yes, thought Marcus. One big happy family.

When poor Jeanette began to backtrack, Marcus let his head fall forward, pinched the bridge of his nose, and took a huge breath. Nausea caught in his stomach. Abruptly pushing his chair back from the table, he stood and addressed Tom's mother and father, interrupting Jeanette. "Moira, John. Thank you very much for this evening. Would love to stay longer, but I need to rush off to deal with an urgent issue."

Under his breath, he muttered, "Get my head examined."

After bidding a general but cursory farewell to everyone—while ignoring eye contact with Tom—Marcus headed out of the restaurant. When he was barely twenty paces along the road, a hand grabbed him by the forearm and spun him around.

"What the hell is wrong with you?" hissed Tom.

"You," cried Marcus, yanking Tom's hand away. Anger bristled inside him, and the raw fury stopped Tom in his tracks. "You're what's wrong with me. Not only are you keeping me out of the loop on things, you've turned me into your dirty little secret. And do you know what's fucking ironic? You're using me for sex and poor clueless Jeanette for respectability. Parading her in front of colleagues, relatives, and teachers because you're too ashamed to have another man by your side. Because of what people might think."

"It's not like that. She's just helping out."

"Are you fucking her?"

"No! There's only you. I told you, we're simply helping each other out. I—I'm doing my best to get things back on an even keel, back to normal."

"Is that what you want? Normal?"

"For the girls' sake, yes. What's so wrong with that?"

"Nothing's wrong with that. It's just…. Where do I fit into your normal?"

The two men stared at each other. Marcus's vision had blurred. Tom had no answer for that, and finally Marcus stepped away from him.

"Just as I thought," he said and then let out a deep sigh before calming his voice. "You know, I think it's my turn now. To tell *you* to *back off*. Give me a chance to find someone who respects me, who can not only be brave enough to stand next to me but also to stand up for me. I'm calling a time-out."

"Is that what you want?"

"Yes. No. *Shit*!" said Marcus, looking out across the street, trying to find the strength to temper his thoughts and emotions. After a deep breath, he brought his gaze back to Tom, his voice softening. "Maybe it's not what I want, but it's what I need. I—I'm in love with you, Tom, I really am. If you don't already know that, then you're blind and deaf. I made a dreadful mistake investigating Damian Stone. Especially after you'd told me quite clearly to drop the idea. I admit that. So if you're doing what you're doing now because of that, then I sort of understand. But I also respect who I am. I've made a name for myself in a tough world. One where I am not only accepted but also—and yes, I know this sounds clichéd—out in the open, and proud of being gay. And I won't live my life settling for the scraps of your life that you're prepared to toss my way. I deserve better than that. And if it means I need to walk away from this, then so be it."

This time Tom glared off into the distance, his eyes glazed. Marcus knew he should act on his words and leave, but he wanted to give Tom a chance to respond. After a few silent moments, he did, but not with anything Marcus wanted to hear. "I don't think you're being fair to Jeanette."

"Oh, for fuck's sake. And are you being fair to me?" cried Marcus. "You've got it all going for you now, haven't you? But you know what? You can't just pick the bits of me that you want and ignore the rest."

"Does that mean the girls won't see you anymore?"

"No," said Marcus, softening his tone. "No, of course not. I said I made a mistake before, and I'm not going to do the same thing again. What I've committed to doing for the girls—helping with homework, taking them to school or picking them up, preparing meals, all of it, I'll keep doing. But you and I need to go back to our previous arrangement, and most definitely stop seeing each other in private. It'll be better that way. Give us both a chance to figure out exactly what we want."

Once again they fell to silence. Even now Tom could not bring himself to look directly at Marcus, his focus on a hole-in-the-wall ATM across the street. Marcus hated seeing his friend appear so lost. His instinct was to pull him into a hug, but with the previous speech still fresh, he knew they had stepped beyond intimacy.

"Go back to the party, Tom. Your parents will be wondering where you are."

Finally Tom folded his arms and swung his gaze back to Marcus. "What do you want, Marcus? Tell me what you want."

"Wrong question, Tom. You need to ask yourself what *you* want. And more importantly, where *my* place is in that."

With that, Marcus turned and walked away.

This time Tom didn't follow.

Chapter Sixteen

TWO weeks later, as a late November chill hit the country, Marcus had seen nothing of Tom Bradford. Whether the man had been purposely avoiding him, he didn't know. Marcus continued to help out and ferry the girls around, even baked a celebratory cake for them all when Katie showed him the B-plus she gained on her school numbers test. But each time, Moira was there to hand over duties. To make matters worse, work had been particularly troublesome, with a sudden wave of staff sickness and then the Birmingham refit, which had stalled because they'd found asbestos in one of the walls.

Add to that the fact that Marcus was no longer getting any sexual release from Tom and he felt as wound tight as the lid of a pickle jar. And what made things worse was that Tom hadn't contacted him—not once. Not even a text message. Yes, Marcus had called the time-out, but the onus was on Tom to make the next move. Unfortunately Marcus had never been good at playing a waiting game—he needed to know where he stood—so that Thursday, he drove over to Tom's to talk, knowing that Thursday was Tom's night in with the girls.

His irritation level ramped up when he found nowhere to park outside the house or along the road, so Marcus finally locked up his car around the corner from the Bradford house. Strolling toward Tom's gave him time to mull over what he wanted to say. Not a bad turn of events, actually, because the walk calmed him down and helped him think things through carefully. However, the minute he turned the corner and saw Jeanette standing at the garden gate, his composure evaporated. Until he realized something was seriously wrong by the way her gaze darted anxiously up and down the road.

As soon as she caught sight of him, her tense expression filled with relief.

"Oh, thank God, Marcus. It's Katie," she said, her face pale as she hurried back into the house. "She's having trouble breathing. Tom had to go to an urgent site meeting, so I said I'd look after her for an hour. We tried her inhaler, but nothing seems to be working."

"Have you called anyone?" said Marcus, striding through the house to the sofa where little Katie lay, her face a bluish tinge. Marcus went straight to her and knelt down. Bless her little soul, she fought to breathe, wheezing horribly, her little chest fighting to gasp for air, rising ridiculously large. Through eyes wide with fright, she momentarily appeared grateful to see Marcus. When Marcus smoothed the hair away from her damp face and propped her up, her body went limp in his hands. She had passed out.

"I called both Tom and Moira. She's picking up Charlotte from ballet class, but neither of them are answering. I left a message," she said.

"Call an ambulance."

"Marcus, I didn't know what to do, she just started—"

"Now, Jeanette! Please. Call them now. Tell them it's an emergency. Tell them Katie's asthmatic. And that she's stopped breathing altogether."

Shocked into action, Jeanette did as asked. For all her hesitation, she had the sense to react to the emergency. Marcus heard her speaking over the phone, cool and unemotional. No doubt she'd had to deal with her own fair share of difficulties with her son. Marcus leaned down and kissed Katie lightly on the forehead.

"Hang in there, baby. Help is on its way."

To see his goddaughter lying there so vulnerable, so helpless, almost broke his heart. But he needed to be strong. For her.

"They'll be here in a couple of minutes," called Jeanette. "St. Mary's is just around the corner."

"How long has she been like this?"

"Just before I saw you. Five or ten minutes. She'd been complaining about being unable to breathe properly since just after I arrived, but said sometimes it just went away. Eventually I got her inhaler, but it didn't seem to have any effect. And then she started gasping for air. So that's when I phoned Moira and Tom. Oh God, Marcus. What's happening?"

"Severe asthma attack. Maybe asthmaticus, I think it's called. One of my kitchen staff in the Edgware Road restaurant has a son that suffers from the same thing. Let's see what the ambulance medics say."

"Should we try mouth-to-mouth?"

"Honestly, I think we should wait for the professionals, Jeanette. I can hear the ambulance siren now. Where's James?"

"With his father and stepmother. That's why I was free to help out at the last minute. Some help, though."

"Nonsense. You did your best."

By the time the ambulance arrived, all color had drained from Katie's face. What Jeanette had told them over the phone had clearly been of great help, because they wheeled in a machine with a hose and translucent mask that they immediately fixed in place over Katie's nose and mouth. Marcus and Jeanette stood by helplessly as the two medics moved quickly but professionally around Katie.

Before long, with a quick curt nod to her partner, the woman broke away and came over to them. "Good thing you called us when you did. We've cleared her airways, so she's breathing normally again and more importantly getting oxygen to the brain. But she's not out of the woods. She's not conscious, so she'll need to be hospitalized immediately."

"Of course," said Marcus.

"Are you the parents?"

"No, we're friends of the family," said Marcus, turning to Jeanette.

"Her father had an urgent meeting to attend. But he'll be on his way back soon."

At that moment Moira appeared at the doorway, flustered and instantly panicked when she saw the scene. Marcus managed to get to her first.

"She's okay, Moira. Well, she's had a severe attack, but she's breathing again. Just not conscious. Can you try calling Tom? Tell him to meet us at the hospital? I think it might be better coming from you."

While Moira—as family—went in the ambulance with Katie, Marcus drove himself and Jeanette to the hospital. Although it was only a few minutes away, the journey took longer because of rush-hour traffic, something the ambulance driver with the blaring siren didn't need to worry about. When they reached the waiting room, Moira sat bolt upright on the plastic chair. Over the past half hour, the poor woman appeared to have aged a decade.

"They've taken her into intensive care. Won't let anyone in until they're satisfied she's stable. But those lovely ambulance people were optimistic."

"Where's Charlotte, Moira?"

"She's at her jazz dance class. Mrs. Kelley's daughter does the same class, so she's going to take Charlie home with them until I call, bless her."

Marcus sat with his head in his hands. All thoughts of having words with Tom had evaporated. How close had they been to losing Katie? No way on earth could Tom have coped with that; even the mere thought made Marcus sick to his stomach. For the next ten minutes they all sat around unspeaking. Nobody could find any words worth uttering. Eventually Moira got up and brought back coffee for them all. As she sat down, an anxious calm descended upon the group.

A calm that was short-lived.

"Where the hell is she? Where's my daughter?" boomed Tom as the doors to the waiting room flew open. All three of them stood on hearing his voice.

"Calm down, dear," said Moira, going to him. "She's in the ICU."

Fortunately a female doctor must have overheard Tom, because she peeled away from a group of orderlies then and went over to him. "Mr. Bradford?"

"Yes. Where's my daughter?"

"We're just getting her settled, so I need to ask you to remain here while we do our work. And I also need information from you about her current doctor and her medical history. After that you can go and see her. Are you okay with that?"

"Fine."

"I'll get someone to bring over the forms."

"Don't worry, dear," said Moira to Tom and the doctor. "I'll come with you and fetch them. Give me something to do."

After watching them head into a small office, Tom swung around and glared at Marcus and Jeanette, his eyes wild with a combination of anger and fear.

"Why didn't you call me sooner?" he said, raising his voice, his face reddened with rage.

"I did. Your phone was switched off."

"Tom," said Marcus, placing a placating hand on his shoulder but having it instantly shrugged away. Tom was wound tight and wanted to vent. "Jeanette did her best."

"That's my daughter in there. Fighting for her life."

Not surprisingly, Jeanette stood in shocked silence, the blood draining from her face. Eventually she shook her head and folded her arms.

"Tom," said Marcus, a little louder this time. People in the waiting room had begun to look over uncomfortably. Even the attendant at the desk appeared to be deciding whether to call someone to intervene. "Reel it in. Jeanette's not to blame here. Katie had a bad asthma attack. It could have happened anywhere, at any time."

"Forty-five minutes I leave her alone," said Tom, his voice still raised, not letting up. "Less than an hour."

Marcus had heard enough.

"You want to blame someone, Tom?" he said assertively, placing himself right in front of Tom until the man had to look him in the eyes. "You want to talk about negligence? How about you start with the father."

"Get out of my face, Marcus."

"No, I will not. Not this time. You're not growling your way out of this one. Everyone is doing their level best to help you out, sacrificing their time to make your life just that little bit easier. And this is the thanks Jeanette gets?"

"I'm warning you."

"You left your daughter, who has a known history of breathing disorders, in the care of someone who is clearly not a medical professional, without giving that person any guidelines or procedures to follow, any numbers to call, any clue of what to do in case of an emergency. You want to blame someone, Tom Bradford? Then why don't you start with yourself."

"That's my family in there, Marcus, my remaining family. They're all I have left in the world. What does it take for people to understand that?" he said, his eyes welling up.

Tom's sudden emotion stopped the words *What about me? Am I not part of your family?* issuing from Marcus's mouth. While the three of them stood there dazed, Moira shuffled up, a clipboard in one hand. She appeared a little flustered and oblivious of the scene that had unfolded only moments earlier.

"Tom, Katie's woken up. The doctor's with her. She's a little shaken up and wants to see you straightaway. Marcus, do you want to—what's happened?"

And just like that, Moira sensed the change in atmosphere. Without a glance or another word to the others, Tom sidestepped her and rushed off toward the ICU.

"Nothing, Moira. Go with Tom. I'll drive Jeanette home."

"But Katie'll want to see you too, Marcus."

Marcus shook his head. "Tomorrow. I'll drop by tomorrow. Once she's had a good night's sleep. She needs her family right now. Go be with her. I'll go pick up Charlotte."

But Moira had not finished and turned to Marcus. "Did Tom start something?"

"No, Moira. Tom didn't start anything. Quite the opposite, actually," said Marcus, trying for a smile that didn't quite reach his eyes. "I'll call you later to find out how Katie's doing. Come on, Jeanette. Let's go."

Enough.

Chapter Seventeen

RAINBOW Voices—a radio station targeted at LGBTQ listeners across the Greater London area—had invited Marcus to join a nighttime chat show a week before Christmas with the ever popular Dr. Billie Rix. Tina had pushed him to do at least three or four of the major commercial stations in London to promote his newly published cookbook. Even though he grumbled because they were live shows and usually meant early mornings or late evenings, he actually enjoyed the anonymity of radio. Rainbow Voices felt like coming home.

On Marcus and Tina's arrival in the cramped studio, sitting outside the fishbowl watching Dr. Rix's animated performance, one of the producers briefed them on the list of questions Marcus might be asked. Phone-ins were a little harder to regulate, but the woman

assured Marcus that any calls would be vetted before
callers were allowed airtime. Marcus had complete
confidence. Being a gay radio station, they probably
had their fair share of hate calls. Tina, as always, had
prepared well ahead with the station and had already
modified some of the content and questions to ensure
Marcus had the opportunity to publicize the book and
his new ventures.

While music played between sections and then the
on-the-hour news was broadcast, Marcus met Dr. Billie
Rix—a beautiful black woman in her early thirties.
Marcus took a shine to her straightaway. Down-to-earth
and authentic, Tina had called her, and she had been
spot-on. After going through a few of the protocols
with him quickly and efficiently, she got straight down
to business on-air.

"You're listening to Rainbow Voices, 92.8 FM, and
this is *Evening Download* with Dr. Billie Rix. With me in
the studio tonight I have the founder and head chef of the
Old Country restaurants, Marcus Vine. Marcus received
recognition from Stonewall in last year's honors as one
of the top twenty most influential gay businesspeople in
the UK. His new book, *Britain's Got Taste*, celebrates
British cuisine across the centuries. Marcus, tell us the
inspiration behind this publication."

"Simple really, Doctor—err—Rix. British cooking
has had a bad rap for far too long, in my humble opinion.
And most of that is unjustified. Ask anyone what they
consider to be classic British dishes and the list won't be
long. Fish and chips, Irish stew, Welsh rarebit, and haggis.
Where's the mention of crempog, rumbledethumps,
cruibini, or good old-fashioned battalia pie, not to mention
a whole encyclopedia of local seafood dishes? We are
an island nation of fishermen, after all. So I decided to

bring these classic dishes, and many more, up-to-date and compiled the recipes in my book. But, of course, if you'd rather not go to all the trouble of recreating them yourself, they're available in any of my restaurants."

Marcus had used the opening lots of times before, one that usually grabbed the attention of listeners. Somebody was bound to ask him about one of the more obscure dishes he had mentioned.

"And if listeners still prefer more popular British dishes?"

"We have variations on those. One of our most popular appetizers is the mini Yorkshire pudding filled with a sliver of sirloin and homemade horseradish. We've simply made them less about bulk and more about taste."

"Some critics accuse you of bending the rules, saying your influences are not restricted to the British Isles. That ingredients used in your recipes are not strictly indigenous."

Aha, thought Marcus. So Dr. BR was not going to give him an easy ride. Fortunately Marcus had heard this kind of objection voiced—usually by competing chefs—many times before.

"Fair enough. But don't forget that Britain has been a pioneering nation since the sixteenth century. Vegetables, fruit, herbs, and spices from all over the world that could either be cultivated here or easily imported became readily available. The potato, for example, originally came over from South America, probably Peru, either brought back by the Spanish or Sir Walter Raleigh—depending on who you believe—and became a mainstay for much of the population. Same goes for the tomato, which is thought to have come to the UK from Spain in the late 1600s. During the age of the Commonwealth, incredible ranges of produce, herbs, and spices came to our shores. Does that make English recipes less authentic? I don't believe so. If anything, it makes them all the more adventurous."

"Okay, we're going to open the switchboard now, so if you have anything at all you'd like to talk about—problems, questions, opinions—with either Marcus or me, we'd be happy to take them. Wouldn't we, Marcus?"

"Whatever you say, Doc."

Dr. Billie Rix laughed then. She had a nice laugh, friendly and open, which probably explained the popularity of her show. "We have Jason on the line. Who's your question for, Jason?"

"For Marcus. Hey there, Marcus."

"Hi, Jason. How can I help?"

"My boyfriend and I have been studying family and consumer sciences for the past two years. We're planning to go into the restaurant trade once we graduate. And you've been a huge inspiration. But my question is a simple one. Neither of us have ever heard of rumbledethumps? What on earth are they?"

Marcus smiled. If only he had a pound for every time somebody asked him the same question. "If you had Scottish relatives, you'd know already. Many countries have their own version, but rumbledethumps is basically a traditional Scottish dish made from potatoes, cabbage, and onion, which is mixed together in a baking dish, seasoned, sprinkled with either cheese or breadcrumbs—depending on whether you're vegetarian stroke vegan—and then baked. I suppose the closest English relative would be bubble and squeak, leftover vegetables from a roast dinner."

"Wow. That simple?"

"Absolutely. But delicious. In my restaurants we offer mini portions as a side dish, or larger ones for sharing. Parents approve because it's popular with the youngsters, even though it contains cabbage."

After allowing a few more calls, Dr. Billie Rix took the reins and started to talk more generally about Marcus. "Marcus," continued Dr. Rix, "congratulations on your award from Stonewall this year. During your modest rise to fame, you've been an inspiration to many young gay people. What's your own coming-out story?"

"Hang on a moment. I can feel another book coming on."

Dr. Rix laughed at the comment, while in the waiting area, Tina nodded enthusiastically and held a thumb in the air.

"I was very lucky. My parents work in theater and television, so they're both liberal and broad-minded and supported me fully when I came out. At school I was never what you'd call macho, but I was taller than most, so perhaps that's why I never got bothered by the big boys. Or maybe it's because my closest friend was the best-looking girl in school and they all thought we were dating. Funny looking back on it now, but I only came out to everyone when I was at university, at the age of twenty. I think I'd known I was gay since the age of twelve. My best friend, Lorraine, certainly did."

"And what piece of advice would you give to any listeners who are struggling with their own sexual identity?"

"Not even my close friends know this, but I used to be terrified of heights. I went out of my way to avoid standing near the edge of anyplace with a big drop because to do so would make me a trembling wreck. Until the age of twenty-two, that is. I joined some college friends on one of those outward-bound camps in North Yorkshire that entailed hiking, canoeing, and other active and supposedly fun stuff. And then one day the instructor split us into four groups and told us that we had team tasks to complete. One of the activities involved each member of our team scaling a cliff face to pick off an envelope with our name on. Unless all members of the team collected their own envelope, however, we would spend the night outside in a flimsy tent, in sleeping bags, on rough terrain, and in whatever conditions the weather brought. Each envelope contained a card with 'gifts' written on them on how comfortably we would spend the night. Things such as cooked food, warm clothes, access to washrooms with hot showers, even alcoholic drinks. But only if every team member picked an envelope would we get to eat in the mess kitchen and sleep in comfortable bunk beds in a cozy dorm.

"Staring up at the cliff face at the darkening sky full of rainclouds, I repeatedly told myself, 'There's no way I can do this.' And then, one by one, my teammates climbed up the cliff and collected envelopes, some just as terrified as me, but all harnessed safely by professionals. The last one remaining, I remember standing there, getting more and more angry with myself, still scared but with the fury getting louder than the fear, at letting my teammates down. So I climbed. And I climbed. And I reached for my envelope just as the heavens opened. And still I climbed until I reached the top of that cliff face and was pulled over the crest by a climbing supervisor, a big bear of a man who wrapped me in a huge hug. Talk about incentive. And when I turned around and looked out through the rain, the view was incredible, and I wondered what the hell I'd been afraid of all this time. For me, that's what coming out was like. Letting my anger overcome my fear and finally seeing things clearly."

"Sign me up for that book. Now I'm sure you've heard a lot of people say that it gets easier. What advice do you have for our listeners?"

"It does. But keep in mind that self-acceptance is only the first step. After that, you need to start living your life. Being true to yourself, being honest about who you are. Standing tall and beating down any self-talk that tells you that you're diminished in any way just because you're different from many of those around you. Diversity is a gift in our society. One person being different from the next makes us stronger, not weaker. We become more interesting and certainly more tolerant of each other. And that can only make for a better society."

"Well said, Marcus. Donald Kitter from the *Observer* called you the best-looking and most eligible gay bachelor in London. Is that still the case?"

"Thanks for that, Dr. BR," said Marcus, his voice softening. "I was seeing someone. Someone very special, actually. But for various reasons, that didn't work out. So I'm keeping my options open. And to be honest, right now I don't get a lot of time for anything but work."

"So what's next, Marcus?"

"Next? My manager and I will probably head back to the restaurant for last knockings. It's not far from here and—" He faltered to a stop when he saw Tina through the thick glass window, rolling her eyes. "Or do you mean my plans for the future?"

"I think listeners are more interested in what the future holds."

"Oh, yes, sorry. Well, I've got my hands full right now with the new restaurant opening in Birmingham at the end of January, but we're always looking for new opportunities."

"No thoughts about doing a television show?"

Marcus could see Tina nodding her head and grinning broadly. She'd set him up. They would have to have words when he was done. "Not sure people want to see my ugly mug on their tellies."

"Oh, Marcus. I don't think there's a single listener on right now who would agree with you on that score. What do you think, Tim?" she said, addressing her sound engineer. "Would you like to watch Marcus live in action on your television?"

Tim, a bald bear of a man, grinned at Marcus and nodded eagerly.

As soon as they went to commercial, Marcus stood up, put his hands on his hips and glared at Tina, who shrugged and tried to look innocent. Fortunately they were approaching the end of the program and he just had to wait for Dr. Billie Rix's trademark sign-off.

"A big Rainbow Voices thank-you to Marcus Vine for being here tonight."

"Thank you for having me."

"Marcus's cookbook, *Britain's Got Taste*, is now available from any high street bookstore or online for the princely sum of £9.99. So if you're anything like me and you've left your Christmas-present shopping until the last minute, this would make a wonderful gift for a loved one. If you want to meet him in person, go along to his book signing in Booklands on Kensington High Street on Boxing Day. And if you happen to find yourself in New York in the near future and long for a taste of home, Marcus's restaurant is now open and getting rave reviews. Details of all his ventures are online at www.marcusvinedining.com. Okay, let's play another topical tune requested by one of our listeners, and definitely one of my favorites. This is 'Ice Cream' by Sarah McLachlan."

Even after Marcus's session has ended, he continued to sit quietly, checking messages on his phone while listening to other callers. Only when he saw Tina stand and hold out her hands, imploring him to come out, did he begin to pack his things. Tina had been uncharacteristically moody of late, and the last thing he wanted to do was irritate her any more. One of the reasons he wanted to head back to the restaurant that night was to have a chat about getting her some help, an assistant, because he felt he had been overstretching her.

Marcus stood up then, seeing that Dr. Rix was almost finished.

"—just enough time for one last call. Who's on the line?"

"Is it okay if I ask a personal question, Dr. Billie Rix?"

In the process of locking up his briefcase, Marcus froze, his throat becoming dry. He would have recognized that voice anywhere. Tom Bradford. Phoning into a chat show. Would wonders never cease?

"Of course. Who's on the line?"

"It's—uh—Thomas."

"Okay, Thomas. Go ahead."

Marcus had received three calls from Tom since their altercation. But each time, he had let them go to voicemail. On the last, Tom had left a simple "Can you please call me back?" Marcus hadn't. And fortunately, Marcus had never found himself alone in a room with Tom. Just as well, because he didn't know if his heart could take another beating. But hearing Tom's voice now, sounding so alone and vulnerable, Marcus found himself missing him, felt tears welling in his eyes.

"Almost two years ago my wife died in a car accident, leaving me with two young daughters to raise."

"Oh, my goodness, Thomas. That's terrible. I'm so sorry to hear."

"Yes, it was a tough time for the family. To begin with, I fell apart and very nearly lost everything. Except that my wife's best friend, a gay man and a dear friend to the family, stepped in to save me, to save us, and basically helped me to rebuild our world. And then something strange happened. I started to develop feelings for this man. Nothing prompted this; the man never showed any interest in me in that way. He had honorable intentions throughout, a friend helping a friend. But I managed to win him over. And eventually our relationship went from one of mutual respect to one of mutual attraction. The relationship also became very physical."

While Tom had been talking, Dr. Billie Rix, noticing Marcus's emotional reaction, had muted her microphone. "You know this man, don't you?"

"Yes."

"Except that I still thought of myself as straight," continued Tom.

"He's talking about you, isn't he?"

"Yes."

"Dr. Rix, do you think it's possible for a straight man to fall in love with a gay man?" asked Tom.

"This is the someone special you—"

"Yes."

After beckoning Marcus back to the interviewer seat, Dr. Billie Rix flicked the microphone back on. "I'd like to think so, Thomas. But let's hear what you think."

"From what I've read, most people think it only happens one way. Gay people falling in love with straight ones."

"And let me tell you on behalf of countless Rainbow Voices listeners, both male and female, we know that particular combination happens all too often. Usually with disastrous results."

In that moment, Marcus realized how much he'd missed hearing Tom's laughter.

"Why do you ask, Thomas?"

"Because earlier in your program, your guest, Marcus Vine, mentioned acceptance. He said it was the first step in coming out, and although I don't yet entirely identify myself as anything other than straight—I haven't been that brave—and while I agree with him, I believe there's something more fundamental. That the whole point of coming out for a lot of people is because eventually they want to be able to have a relationship, maybe even be lucky enough to build a life, with another person. Everyone, gay or straight, wants to love and be loved. It's a basic human need. But we are never going to respect a potential partner if we're not brave enough to respect ourselves, to understand that what we're gaining is so much more than what we lose. And I know this because that's where I fell short.

"I am not a complicated man. I could easily remain the way I am, unexceptional but conventional, continue to live my life through work and through my daughters as a widower. Because I know now that there will never be another woman to replace my wife. And I also know that many men and women in my shoes manage to continue living on alone and single when their spouse passes on. But for me that would be worse than shutting myself in a closet. Because I've been given a rare gift, sent a second soul mate who unconditionally loved me and my family, who has already supported us through the good times and especially the bad. Someone I let down because I wasn't brave enough to tell him I loved him, and someone I eventually pushed away. So my question is this: Do you think a man who lacked courage and respect, but who has learned his lesson and would never do the same again, who promises to stand proud next to the person—to the man—he loves with all his heart, could be worth a second chance?"

"Marcus is still with us, Thomas," came the voice of Dr. Billie Rix. "Marcus, do you think someone like Thomas could be worth a second chance?"

Marcus peered through the glass paneling to where Tina sat, a handkerchief balled up over her mouth, her eyes pooling with tears. Of course he had told her all about Tom. When she caught his eye, she nodded vigorously, sending tears spilling down her cheek.

"I do," choked Marcus. "Yes, Tom. I do."

Chapter Eighteen

COLD rain fell unceasingly from the night sky on their stroll back to the restaurant. Both huddled beneath their umbrellas, both unspeaking, Marcus repeatedly checking his phone, wondering if Tom would call or text. Finally, when a ping came through, he stopped walking and stared down at the display.

Tom.

I need to see you. If you'll let me.

Marcus texted back immediately.

Of course I will. I'm off all day tomorrow.

Good. This can't wait.

"Tom?" asked Tina, who had stopped and turned back a few paces in front.

"Yes," he said, staring first at the phone display and then at Tina.

"And?"

"He wants to talk," he said as he caught up and continued on toward the restaurant. "Tomorrow."

"And how do you feel about that?"

"I'm not sure. But I did say I'd give him a second chance, didn't I?"

Countless thoughts swam around his head as they moved onward. Was he doing the right thing? Would meeting up change anything? One thing was for certain. Without Tom in his life, he felt more miserable than ever. When they reached the restaurant door, Marcus stopped and turned to Tina.

"You can head off now, if you want. I'll help finish up in the kitchen."

"No," she said firmly. "I need to talk to you too. About me. Come on, let's go to your office and get a couple of drinks."

Something about her tone put him on guard. And then, once they'd sat down and one of his team had asked them what they wanted to eat and drink, she shocked him again. In all the years he had known Tina, she had never refused a glass of red wine in favor of mineral water. Certainly not after such an exhausting day. Without speaking, she sat waiting patiently for him to finish a roast beef sandwich and a bottle of beer. After what she had said, he had begun to think the worst, that she was going to quit.

He couldn't have been further from the truth.

"You're what?"

"I'm pregnant."

They sat in his small office with the door open while his kitchen staff went about cleaning up. He would have sat them both outside in the main restaurant, but four tables were still occupied with regulars finishing their coffees and liqueurs. Besides, his staff had been listening to his interview, and every now and then, one of them popped their head in to give him a thumbs-up.

"Oh my goodness," said Marcus, getting up from his seat and going around to give her a hug. "That's fantastic."

"You're not mad?"

"Why on earth would I be mad?"

"Because I'll need to take time off."

"Come on, Tina. You know me better than that. You've worked tirelessly for me all these years. We would never have been half as successful without your hard work and without you pushing me to do more. I am so happy for you and Mel. How far along are you?"

"Two months."

"Sex?"

"That's generally how it's done."

"Of the baby, smartass."

"We don't know yet. But we're hoping for a girl."

"A little Tina. Brilliant. And perfect timing. Because I was going to ask if you needed me to hire you an assistant to help you with everything. You've been so overloaded of late. Now it'll be a must and you'll even have time to train them up."

"Uh, Marcus," said Michelle, the head waiter, standing in the doorway, looking puzzled. "Sorry to disturb. But there's some big guy out front, says he needs to speak to you. Urgently."

Marcus and Tina looked quizzically at each other.

"Couldn't be, could it?" asked Marcus.

But it was. Tom stood in the middle of the restaurant. He appeared not only lost, but also terrified. Togged out in a donkey jacket, a yellow-and-mauve striped rugby shirt, and jeans, hands shoved in his pockets, he had clearly gotten there in a hurry. And the way his eyes darted fearfully around the remaining guests, he looked like the accused. Maybe against his better judgment, Marcus wanted to go up to him and give him a hug.

"Come through to the kitchen," said Marcus, beckoning him over.

"No," said Tom firmly. "I need to do this out here. In public."

"Are you absolutely sure?"

"Yes."

"Okay."

After a long pause, during which Tom's brows repeatedly scrunched together and his eyes brimmed wetly, he finally uttered one word, one single word.

"Anything."

"I'm sorry, Tom. I don't understand."

"I'll give you anything. Anything you want. If you can just love me. What I did was unforgivable, I know, pushing you away again. Yet here I am asking for a forgiveness that I don't really deserve. But I'm prepared to do anything you want to bring you back."

Diners at two of the tables had stopped talking and were watching them with interest.

"Tom, we can take this out back."

"No," he said firmly, still unmoving. "I don't care if people hear. I *want* them to. I don't care anymore. I love you. And I hurt you. But I meant every word I said on the radio. I need you, Marcus. You're my soul mate. I'm nothing without you. But I can't move forward until you tell me—"

But Tom couldn't get the words out and broke down, bowing his head. Marcus strode forward and pulled Tom's head onto his shoulder, barely hearing the round of applause that went up from the tables. When

Marcus cupped Tom's chin in his hand and raised Tom's head, he brought their lips together and tasted salty tears. Slowly, Tom's dangling arms came to life and wrapped snugly around Marcus's waist.

"Of course I forgive you, you pillock," said Marcus, kissing the soft skin of Tom's neck that he had always loved. By now he had forgotten the audience. "Hey, who's looking after the girls?"

"Jeanette. I've made my peace with her too. You were right on all counts."

"What if Katie has another episode?"

"All taken care of," said Tom, smoothing his cheek against Marcus's chin. "With the help of the hospital, we've bought a portable device that helps clear the lungs in an emergency, and I've put simple instructions how to use it up on the fridge door for anyone to read."

"Even me?"

"Yes, even you," said Tom, a hint of a smile rubbing against Marcus's cheek. "See? Your message finally got through my thick skull. I also came clean to Jeanette about us. Only fair, really. And she's been a star. So anyway, I told her what I needed to do tonight, and she said she'd stay until we got home."

"We?"

Tom pulled his face away from Marcus and stared deep into his eyes.

"I want you to come home with me, Marcus. Tonight, if possible. But only if you want to. And if you do, I want you in my bed tonight. I want to wake up in the morning with you next to me and let the girls see us together. I'll even take the day off tomorrow so that we can take them to school. Together. And later on we can go see Mum and Dad. Tell them about us. Not everyone's going to understand or be happy—especially my football friends and work buddies. But that's their problem. I can deal with anything. As long as I have you by my side. As long as I have your forgiveness."

"I've already said you have that. But we need to communicate better in the future, Tom."

"What do you mean?"

"Tell each other things, especially feelings, and not leave each other to guess. I'm here for the long haul, a permanent fixture not just for the girls, but for you. To organize the house, meet the teachers, put up Christmas decorations, cook for you without you feeling as though it's a chore for me. Someone you can trust never to simply up and disappear when times get tough. That's not me."

"I know," said Tom, smiling gently. "I really do. But there's only one thing I need right now."

"And what's that?"

"You."

Marcus took a moment while he held Tom's gaze.

"You've always had me."

Epilogue

"OVER my dead body," said Moira, the disgust plain on her face.

"Mother, it's my choice—"

"It's not a choice," she cried. "It's an abomination."

"Mum—"

"No, Tom. Absolutely not. I will not allow it."

"Even if it's what I want?" pleaded Tom. Although Marcus was pleased to see Tom keep his temper under control, he wanted to wade in. Instead, he stood in the background, unspeaking, lending solidarity but not interfering—as explicitly instructed.

"What about what *I* want?" said Moira, her voice almost cracking. "What about what our relatives will say, let alone the neighbors and the ladies of the conservative club? It's disgusting. You have my support on most things,

Thomas Jonathan Bradford, but not this. As for you, Marcus, I'm shocked and disappointed. Surely you of all people can see how wrong this is. Can't you talk some sense into my son?"

"Actually, Moira—"

"Marcus," said Tom, gently but firmly, "we agreed. This is my decision to make. Let me deal with my mother."

"What have the girls said?"

"I wanted to get your blessing first of all."

"Katie will disown you."

"Ooh, come on, Mrs. B," hissed Marcus. "That's a bit strong."

"Marcus. Please stay out of this."

"I'm not backing down, Thomas. No son of mine—" began Moira.

"Oh, for goodness' sake, woman," interrupted John sternly, wheeling in from the living room. He had clearly been trying to read the newspaper sitting open in his lap and been disturbed by the constant bickering. "It's his life. Let him do what makes him happy."

"What about *my* happiness? What about *our* respectability?"

An uneasy calm fell between the four of them. Eventually Marcus took a huge sigh and decided to step into the fray to break the stalemate.

"Look, I know nobody's asked my opinion. But on this occasion, I actually agree with Moira. Every step of the way."

Both John and Tom turned on Marcus then. Tom was the first to speak.

"You... what? What do you mean?"

"Powder blue with white trim is simply not your color, Tom. I've never seen such an awful-looking tux in my life.

And are the white patent leather shoes for real? Even with the navy cummerbund and bow tie, which, I admit, add a teaspoonful of class, it's the epitome of Tack-A-Rama. Like a 1970s game show host or someone who's stepped off the set of the original *Ocean's Eleven* movie."

"Thank you, Marcus," said Moira, folding her arms. "I'm glad one of you has some sense of decency."

"I loved that movie," muttered John.

"Hang on," said Tom. "You said it was fabulous? In the charity shop?"

Marcus came over then, put his arm around Tom's waist, and lightly kissed him on the cheek. Even after four years, with Marcus doing his damnedest to suggest fashion choices for Tom, the man still showed up in some absolute doozies.

"It was fabulous in the charity shop. But that's where it should have stayed. There's a good reason it was there in the first place. Anyway, Mum's right. You should wear your black tux to the party. With the simple white wingtip and black bow tie."

"Boring."

"You still have no idea, do you? Quite how incredibly hot—I mean, *handsome*—you look in that combination. Maybe that's a good thing."

"What? And I don't look incredibly hot and handsome in this? Come on, Dad. What do you think?"

"Okay, son. Marcus has a point. It *is* a bit gay."

"John!"

"Dad!"

Moira and Tom spoke in horrified unison, while Marcus collapsed into fits of laughter. Eventually everyone followed suit, bringing Katie into the room to find out what all the fuss was about. At twelve now, she had grown all too quickly.

"What are you all—? *Oh* my *God*, Dad. What *are* you wearing?"

Behind her, Charlotte burst into loud, uncontrollable fits of giggles, starting the whole room off again—until the front doorbell rang.

"Heavens," said Moira, checking her watch. "Is that the time already? For goodness' sake, go up and change, Tom. I'll let the guests in."

Marcus had been pleasantly surprised at how quickly the Bradfords had come around to their son's feelings for Marcus. Moira had been a tough sell at first, but having had Marcus in their lives for so long made things that much easier. Three months after the announcement, Moira had quietly spoken to Marcus as she turned up at his apartment to collect the girls.

"I'm not going to say that I understand. But my granddaughters adore you and my son has been the happiest he's ever been since his wife died. So. That's all I'm going to say on the matter."

Case closed.

Both girls had been overjoyed, but for the first couple of months, even though Marcus had spent most nights in Tom's bed, they had been careful. Sunday mornings especially, they'd been regularly invaded by the girls jumping up and down on their mattress and scaring Marcus awake. But that was a small price to pay. When Marcus went to pick Charlotte up from school one day and overheard her referring to him as "…my other dad. He's famous, you know?", he felt such a sense of pride— he texted Tom as soon as they'd gotten home.

Marcus suspected that Tom felt the brunt more than he. At one point Tom had almost given up on going down to the pub with his football chums, until Marcus had persuaded him that he had every right to be there.

Perry, whose wife, Julia, and kids had been close to Tom's family, had been the hardest cold shoulder to take. When Tom announced the news, Perry became distant, purposely avoiding talking to Tom. Whenever they did, usually just a few words, they'd talk about the kids or football—nothing too emotive. Maybe time and patience would help, but on more than one occasion, Tom stated openly that he had gained more than he had lost.

And now here they were, four years later, Tom at forty-five, Marcus at thirty-five, about to celebrate their combined eightieth birthday party together. Had she been alive, Raine would have wanted this.

Fitting over a hundred people into the back garden of their new semidetached house turned out to be easier than either of them imagined. Fortunately Marcus and Tom's new neighbors had all accepted the invitation to their garden party, so they could at least continue into the early July evening while daylight remained. More importantly, they had woken to cloudless blue skies and a beautiful summer temperature, although weather reports hinted at showers. To prepare for all possibilities, Tina had gotten Joel, her latest assistant, to call her events contacts and book a large marquee, which they had erected at one end of their spacious garden. Even rain could not have stopped the event. As it turned out, John, Moira, and Marcus's parents, Colin and Debs, who turned up later, appreciated being able to sit in the shade.

Since Tom, Marcus, and the girls had moved into the house two roads away from John and Moira, life had settled into a comfortable rhythm.

Late in the afternoon of the party, with Tom uncharacteristically insisting on providing the speech to all gathered—despite Marcus's offer to take over—

Marcus stood at the sink of their kitchen, the window open, enjoying the aroma from his small window-ledge herb garden. After sending the girls off to collect used plates, cups, cutlery, and glasses from around the garden, Marcus washed while Moira wiped.

"Even when Lorraine was alive, I was always going to be in their lives, Moira. That much hasn't changed," said Marcus, rinsing tumblers one by one, then handing them absently to Moira. "You know. Background checks on the girls' dates when the princesses grew old and serious enough to go on them, even if that entailed hiring private detectives. Or a personal stakeout outside their respective houses."

Beside him, Moira clucked her tongue the way she did when John had said something politically incorrect. And there across the garden lawn, the man himself— John—sat holding court as usual, laughing with a cluster of relatives and friends, all enjoying the afternoon and the company. Behind him, Lincoln Prescott used his hands to talk animatedly about something with an out-of-uniform Daniel Mosborough and Ken Villers, Damian Stone's widower. Beneath their cherry tree, Marcus's bookkeeper, Trevor, who had recently had a difficult split from his long-term partner, stood in complete awe with a towering Kim Kendrick, their New York investor. Marcus always had a warm feeling when everything felt right with the world, when different friends or associates of his found common ground.

"And now I'll have Tom by my side through good times and bad. And I honestly can't think of anything more wonderful. A couple of curly straws, sharing a can of Special Brew in the old folks' home together while we watch Chelsea version 255 with players whose names neither of us can remember. Or sitting on the front pew at St. Mark's with you and other members of the family while Tom walks one of his beauties down the aisle. Or being there to hug the man and stuff a cigar in his mouth when one of them produces a grandson or granddaughter."

Absently, he twisted his head around and for the first time in his life saw Moira had turned away from him. For a moment he wondered what was happening, thought she might have turned away to sneeze, until he noticed a small movement, the gentle rise and fall of her back. She was sobbing. Unsure what to do, he dried his hands quickly and put his arm around her shoulders.

"I'm so sorry, Moira," he said, mortified. "I didn't realize—"

"Oh, don't mind me, dear," she said, pulling away, embarrassed at herself, wiping her eyes with the tea towel. Straightening up, she patted him on the forearm, back to her old starchy self. "Just getting a little soppy in my old age. Shush, anyway. Tom's about to give his speech."

Instantly Marcus strolled out through the kitchen door to join the crowd and watch the love of his life standing alone on the small stage. In that moment, his stomach curdled. He knew how nervous Tom was at speaking publicly. Tom had tried to memorize the speech over and over. And now the time had come.

"Family and friends, neighbors and—and—guests. Welcome to our garden party to celebrate our combined eightieth birthday. I'm not going to let on to our individual ages, but just let you guess. However, please remember that Marcus has misleadingly young genes. Today is also a time to commemorate someone who has meant such a lot to many of us gathered. My late wife once planned to have a joint birthday party for me and her best friend, something she never lived to see. So a big part of today is fulfilling her wish."

Tom stopped for a moment, overcome, and Marcus put the tea towel down, ready to go and help him. But then he rallied.

"I know it's me giving the speech today when Marcus could probably do this with his eyes closed. But I wanted to prove to him—and to myself—that I can do this. Sometimes we all need to take a step outside our comfort zone, to appreciate what others do for us and also to help us become stronger. That is something Marcus taught me, and I am so grateful to him for that as well as a host of other things. I am also grateful for my parents being close at hand, for my darling Katie, who is growing up so fast and, more importantly, has settled into her studies and is doing her dad and Marcus proud at grammar school. To Charlie, who used to dance like an angel and now dances like—"

"Beyoncé!"

The crowd laughed, which seemed to relax Tom even more.

"I was going to say Madonna, but Beyoncé will do."

"Dad!" shouted Charlotte from somewhere in the crowd, followed by the muttered "so embarrassing."

"But who has always, somehow, been able to put a smile onto anyone's lips. Especially grumpy old Granddad's."

Tom continued on thanking family, his people at work for being supportive, and his friends for turning out that day, even giving a special mention to Marcus's parents, who had traveled a long way to join them. Eventually, having fluffed a few lines—nothing serious—he reached the toast.

"So finally, I would like to toast a propose—" said Tom, then quickly clammed up. Many of those gathered chuckled at Tom's faux pas.

Marcus willed Tom to keep going, his heart going out to Tom. "Come on, love," Marcus muttered to himself. "You can do this. You would like to propose a toast to all those gathered here on our joint eightieth birthday party."

"Wait, no," said Tom, an uncomfortable feedback screech coming from the personal address system. "This is coming out all wrong."

Marcus stared above the heads of the crowd, willing Tom to say what he needed.

"I would like to—"

Once again Tom stuttered to a halt. Marcus quickly wiped his hands and began to stride toward Tom. All those gathered parted as Marcus headed for the small stage.

"Shit, where's Marcus?" said Tom.

"Don't worry," called Marcus. "The cavalry's here. Hold your horses."

"Should have done this years ago," said Tom, still speaking into the microphone. "I would like to propose, Marcus."

"I know," said Marcus, reaching the stage. "You'd like to propose a toast to all those gathered here today on our combined eightieth birthday."

"No," said Tom, a self-assured smile Marcus had rarely seen spreading across his face. And just like that, Tom dropped onto one knee. "I would like to propose. To you. Will you, Marcus Edward Vine, marry me?"

With that, Tom revealed the small velvet box he had been holding. Marcus barely heard the cheer that went up around the garden, followed by a huge round of applause. With tears in his eyes, he stared bleary-eyed into Tom's happy face.

And with that, a drop fell onto Marcus's hand. Oddly, the spot felt cold, not the warm teardrop he had expected. And then, speck by speck, more cold spots touched his arm, his forehead, his nose, his lips—until finally he realized what was happening.

Rain.

Coming in September 2018

ⓓREAMSPUN DESIRES

Dreamspun Desires #65
Two of a Kind by BA Tortuga

Working on a full house.

Once upon a time, Trey Williamson and Ap McIntosh had quite the whirlwind romance—but that was before family tragedy left them the guardians of five kids. Their lives have changed quite a bit over the last six years, but Ap is still on the rodeo circuit, doing what he does best in an attempt to feed all those extra mouths.

That leaves Trey back on the ranch, isolated and overworked as the kids' sole caregiver. Something has to give, and when Ap comes home, they're reminded how hot they burned once upon a time. But is it a love that can withstand wrangling over time, money, and the future? They have to decide what kind of family they want to be… and whether what they share can stand the test of time.

Dreamspun Desires #66
The Nerd and the Prince by B.G. Thomas

A Small-Town Dreams Story

Prince Charming is the man next door.

Small-town business owner Jason Brewster has big dreams: world travel, adventure, and most of all, a passionate romance worthy of a fairy tale. But he doesn't believe fantasies can come true….

Until Adam moves in next door.

He's handsome, cultured, European, and best of all, interested in Jason. It's like something out of the stories Jason loves.

But Adam—whose real name is Amadeo Montefalcone—has a secret. He's royalty, prince of the small country of Monterosia. Only he doesn't want to rule, and especially doesn't want the loveless marriage waiting for him at home. So he ran away in search of true love. With a man. And with Jason, he finds it.

But Adam can't run forever. The truth will come out. If Jason can forgive Adam's deception, they might find their happily ever after.

Now Available

Dreamspun Desires #61
Stranger in a Foreign Land by Michael Murphy

Losing his old life and finding a new love.

After an accident stole his memory, the only home American businessman Patrick knows is Bangkok. He recovers under the tender ministrations of Jack, an Australian expat who works nights at a pineapple cannery. Together they search for clues to Patrick's identity, but without success. Soon that forgotten past seems less and less important as Jack and Patrick—now known as Buddy—build a new life together.

But the past comes crashing in when Patrick's brother travels to Thailand looking for him… and demands Patrick return to Los Angeles, away from Jack and the only world familiar to him. The attention also causes trouble for Jack, and to make their way back to each other, Patrick will need to find not only himself, but Jack as well, before everything is lost….

Dreamspun Desires #62
A Fool and His Manny by Amy Lane

Seeing the truth and falling in love.

Dustin Robbins-Grayson was a surly adolescent when Quinlan Gregory started the nanny gig. After a rocky start, he grew into Quinlan's friend and confidant—and a damned sexy man.

At twenty-one, Dusty sees how Quinlan sacrificed his own life and desires to care for Dusty's family. He's ready to claim Quinlan—he's never met a kinder, more capable, more lovable man. Or a lonelier one. Quinlan has spent his life as the stranger on the edge of the photograph, but Dusty wants Quinlan to be the center of his world. First he has to convince Quinlan he's an adult, their love is real, and Quinlan can be more than a friend and caregiver. Can he show Quin that he deserves to be both a man and a lover, and that in Dusty's eyes, he's never been "just the manny?"